Batmaof
mist and found nothing but shadows. He gave a chok-
ing cough as smoke from the blazing exhibits swirled
down to mix with the dissipating mist. He stumbled
back through the charred debris. Then the burning
globe exploded with a roar, sending out a wall of intense heat that broke over him like a wave. He flung
his arms up to protect his face and took a blind step
backward.

The ground opened up beneath him . . .

man threw himself forward into the clouds

MASK OF THE PHANTASM

BATMAN™

THE ANIMATED MOVIE

A Novelization by Geary Gravel

Based on an original story by Alan Burnett

WARNER BROS. Presents
KEVIN CONROY MARK HAMILL DANA DELANY HART BOCHNER ABE VIGODA
Co-Producers ALAN BURNETT ERIC RADOMSKI and BRUCE W. TIMM
Executive Producer TOM RUEGGER Produced by BENJAMIN MELNIKER and MICHAEL USLAN
Based on DC Comics characters Batman created by BOB KANE
Story by ALAN BURNETT Screenplay by ALAN BURNETT PAUL DINI MARTIN PASKO and MICHAEL REAVES
Sequence Directors KEVIN ALTIERI BOYD KIRKLAND FRANK PAUR & DAN RIBA
Music by SHIRLEY WALKER Directed by ERIC RADOMSKI & BRUCE W. TIMM

BANTAM BOOKS
NEW YORK · TORONTO · LONDON · SYDNEY · AUCKLAND

BATMAN: MASK OF THE PHANTASM
A Bantam Book / January 1994

*Batman and all related characters, slogans, and indicia are
trademarks of DC Comics*

Produced by RHK Creative Services

ISBN 0-553-56581-8

Published simultaneously in the United States and Canada

*This book is intended for sale only in the United States of America, its territories
and dependencies, the Republic of the Philippines and Canada.*

*Bantam Books are published by Bantam Books, a division of Bantam Doubleday Dell
Publishing Group, Inc. Its trademark, consisting of the words "Bantam Books" and
the portrayal of a rooster, is Registered in U.S. Patent and Trademark Office and in
other countries. Marca Registrada. Bantam Books, 1540 Broadway, New York, New
York 10036.*

PRINTED IN THE UNITED STATES OF AMERICA

OPM   0   9   8   7   6   5   4   3   2   1

ONE

Night was settling its dark cloak over Gotham City. The last colorful streaks of sunset had vanished, and tiny stars shone dimly through a high haze compounded of moisture and pollution. A few wisps of pale cloud clung like tattered garments to the tallest skyscrapers.

On a grinning stone gargoyle that protruded like an unplanned outcropping near the summit of a man-made spire of concrete and steel, a lone figure stood looking upward at the blurred points of light.

The man was garbed in the colors of the night and the night accepted his presence. When he turned from the stars and leaned forward on the ugly stone head to stare at the city below, his motions were barely perceptible, lost in the shadows that surrounded him.

Traffic moved fitfully in the maze of streets and alleyways below him. The business districts which had hummed with commerce during the day were nearly silent now, their towering office buildings dark, while

BATMAN: THE ANIMATED MOVIE

certain other sections of the city were just shaking themselves awake. The bookie joints and casinos, the dance halls and all-night movie houses moved to their own feverish rhythm, a twitch and a jangle unrelated to the ordered pulse of the day. Slitted eyes searched the sprawl of garish lights and blinking neon, coming to rest on a tall, well-lit building whose roof bore the outline of a thirty-foot cutout of a woman, posed provocatively with one hand on her hip and the other behind her head.

The man reached behind him for something resting on the gargoyle's broad skull. His gloved hands made adjustments to an oddly shaped construction of thin metal struts and panels of dark fabric. Then he rose to his feet, took a deep breath, and launched himself out into the space between the buildings. For a moment he was lost, invisible among the shadowed canyons.

Seconds later, a black-winged shape swooped out of the darkness, falling with the exquisite control of a hunting bird until it landed silently on the roof of the Shady Lady Casino, just behind the well-turned left ankle of the seductively smiling giant caricature.

The dark-clad man released himself from the glider and straightened slowly, his eyes searching the shadows. His boots crunched softly as he prowled the rooftop, his cowled head cocked in a listening attitude. A rectangular skylight was set into the roof. The man chose a particular spot not far from the angled panes of glass and removed a small device from a hidden compartment in his belt. There was a muffled report as he fired a black dart into the surface of the roof.

MASK OF THE PHANTASM

The portion of the dart protruding from the tarmac resembled a slender antenna.

The man pulled an earphone from his belt and held it to the side of his black hood.

"Go ahead, boys, take a good close look . . ." said a gravelly voice in his ear. The man in the black mask smiled a small grim smile.

The Shady Lady Casino occupied the first three stories of the recently renovated structure once home to the Gotham City Venetian Blind Laundry and now known as the Hotel Grand Imperator.

The penthouse suite of the Grand Imperator was both plush and tawdry, from its gold lamé wallpaper to the sunken entertainment pit where purple velour cushions surrounded a wide-screen TV. The main room of the suite featured a conference table embellished with carvings of mermaids and a pseudomarble fountain gurgling at the center of a sea of scarlet carpeting. To facilitate business transactions, a fully stocked bar covered one entire wall of the suite.

The current occupant of the Grand Imperator's penthouse was one Charlton "Chuckie" Sol, a squat, pale-skinned man whose involvement with organized crime stretched back over thirty-five of his fifty-odd years of life.

At the moment, Sol was standing at the head of the conference table, a medium-sized briefcase open on the table in front of him. Four men sat at the table, the smoke from their cigars hanging like a blue veil beneath the gold cupids of the chandelier.

"Go ahead," Sol said again to the four men seated

BATMAN: THE ANIMATED MOVIE

at the table. He tapped the side of the briefcase. "Dive in!" The briefcase was filled with neat stacks of hundred-dollar bills.

One by one the men leaned in. Each withdrew a stack of bills.

"Jeez, Mr. Sol." The hoodlum closest to the head of the table squinted at one of the hundreds, rubbing its surface with his blunt fingertip. "I can't tell the difference between this and a *real* one."

Sol beamed in satisfaction. "Course ya can't," he rasped. "You'd need one a' them nuclear microscopes." Thirty-five years of smoke-filled rooms had left Chuckie Sol with a voice that approximated the sound of a cement mixer badly in need of an overhaul. "It's identical right down to ol' Ben Franklin's chin stubble." He held out his hand and collected the stacks from his henchmen, counting silently under his breath. He carefully replaced the last bill and stepped back from the table, one eye on the briefcase as he crossed to the bar and poured himself a glass of amber liquid. There was a slight flicker of movement in the darkness beyond the large window that looked out over Gotham. Sol returned to the table and scowled at his henchmen, his manner businesslike.

"I want the dough laundered through the casino at a half million a week. Three-quarters of a mil by March. Anybody got a problem with that?"

The answer came with a crash of glass as the huge picture window shattered inward. The thugs stumbled back from the table, arms raising instinctively to shield their faces as a dark figure swung into the room on a slender line.

MASK OF THE PHANTASM

Chuckie Sol gasped in astonishment. The man who landed lightly on his feet on the glass-strewn carpet was tall and strongly muscled, dressed in a form-fitting uniform of gray with black boots and gloves. A segmented gold belt was clasped around his flat middle, and a golden emblem glinted from his broad chest, where it framed the stylized image of a black bat suspended in flight. A cowl that rose into two stiff points and a long, scalloped black cape echoed the motif of a winged denizen of the night. The face beneath the black mask was grim.

"The Bat!" Sol yelled, an edge of hysteria cracking in his rough voice. "*Nail* 'im!"

The four hoodlums reached for their guns. A pair of small black objects appeared in the masked man's hand and went whirring across the room. Two of the thugs on opposite sides of the conference table cried out and clutched their hands as their pistols went flying. The largest of the crooks stuffed his own gun back in his pocket with a contemptuous snort and lumbered toward the intruder, ham-sized fists ready to swing.

Batman ducked easily beneath the first punch. His own black-gloved fist rocketed toward the thug's lantern jaw. As the big man staggered back, the Dark Knight delivered an uppercut that propelled the crook onto the conference table and sent him sliding down its length, empty bottles and half-filled ashtrays flying off to either side.

Chuckie Sol swooped in to yank the briefcase out of his hireling's glide path, snapping it shut in a smooth motion as he tucked it under his arm.

Both of the men who had been disarmed earlier had retrieved their weapons. They jockeyed for a clear shot as the fourth man bobbed and weaved toward Batman. The Dark Knight shook his head reprovingly. "You guys just don't get it, do you?" he said. As the nearest man took a swing at him, he leaped to one side, reached inside his cape, and sent a third black batarang whirring past his sparring partner toward his other prey. The bat-shaped missile knocked the gun from one crook's hand, ricocheted across the table, and struck the shorter man a glancing blow on the side of the head. As the little man reeled from the impact, Batman grabbed him and flipped him through the air to land on top of his partner, who was kneeling to grope for his weapon. The two crashed backward into a display case filled with small glass statuettes of famous ecdysiasts.

The fourth man had raced around to the head of the conference table. Now he pulled his own gun and aimed at the gray-and-black figure. "Don't worry, guys," he growled to his confederates. "I can't miss at this range."

The first bullet whined an inch from the bat mask's pointed left ear. Abruptly the Dark Knight lunged forward, ducked low, and disappeared under the long table. The second shot punched a fist-sized hole between two mermaids in the expensive mahogany. Panic growing in his eyes, the crook fired shot after shot into the dark wood. Batman braced his shoulders against the underside of the massive table, then straightened suddenly, heaving the table into the air. The crook stared in frozen wonderment at the slab of wood as it hung poised, then toppled down on top of him with a shuddering crash.

Chuckie Sol had begun edging toward the doorway as he watched the commencement of battle. Sensing the imminent defeat of his men when the Dark Knight threw his first batarangs, Sol had clutched the briefcase to his chest and bolted out into the corridor.

As Batman turned toward the door, a heavy hand fell on his shoulder from behind. The Dark Knight turned with a *tsk* of annoyance, lightly sidestepping a vicious right. His eyes still on his destination, he elbowed the large thug in his ample midsection, grasped his jacket at collar and hem, and sent the man flying toward the nearest patch of gold wallpaper. The hoodlum struck a portrait of a scantily clad actress with platinum hair, dropped heavily onto a low bookshelf lined with cheap crime novels, and rolled onto the carpeted floor with a moan. Batman made a quick survey of the room.

Finding no one else in any condition to follow him, he exited the suite in pursuit of the runaway Sol.

TWO

Chuckie Sol dashed across the open-air bridge that connected the penthouse level of the Grand Imperator with the top story of the neighboring parking garage. He was puffing with exertion by the time he reached the shadowy cavern of the garage. He paused at the entranceway to look back over his shoulder. No sign of the Dark Knight. He took a moment to catch his breath, then ducked inside.

His car was parked in the lot reserved for special customers on the roof of the garage. He searched the gloom for the nearest stairwell and took off toward it, the briefcase banging against his thigh as he loped across the concrete floor.

Then he saw it.

Sol skidded to a halt and looked frantically to either side. There had to be other stairs!

About fifty yards in front of him, directly between him and the stairwell to the roof, stood a shadowy figure in a long dark cloak. Swirls of smoky mist surrounded the figure, clinging to it in dark tendrils as it began to move slowly toward him.

"*Chuckie Sol . . .*"

Sol blanched. The voice had a weird, computer-altered quality to it that sent a chill up the gangster's backbone. "Batman!" he cried, whipping out his gun. He fired five shots in rapid succession.

The bullets seemed to have no effect, disappearing harmlessly one by one into the swirls of mist that obscured the figure. The apparition continued to move toward him, gliding smoothly as if floating on the mist that surrounded it. Its ragged black cloak fluttered behind it.

"*Your angel of death awaits you, Sol,*" the menacing voice intoned. The gangster's eyes grew wide as the cloaked figure passed under one of the garage's dim lights and he saw the pale skull mask that rode upon its shoulders. "*Gaze upon your death mask. . . .*"

Sol's pistol clicked on empty chambers. "You ain't the Bat!" he grated. "Why're you—"

With a sudden rush of speed, the dark figure glided in, raised its right arm from beneath its cloak, and knocked the gun out of his hand. Sol gaped as he watched the shiny metal spin across the concrete floor. The pistol had been neatly sliced in two.

His eyes darted back to the black figure. A wickedly curved, foot-long blade glinted at the end of the black-draped right arm. Sol cowered back in terror as the apparition raised its gloved left arm and backhanded him. The gangster went flying, the briefcase dropping from his hand as he crashed back against a concrete pylon. He slumped to the ground, feeling a warm trickle of blood beginning at the corner of his lip.

"Who—what are you?" He scrambled to his feet as the dark figure glided toward him. "Whaddya want from me?"

With unexpected strength, the skull-headed figure grabbed him by the lapels and hoisted him into the air, slamming his back and shoulders against the pylon. Sol cried out in pain and fright.

The two stood nose to nose in the dimness, the sharp inward-curving jut of the skull's gaping nostrils pressing against Sol's skin. *"I want* you, *Chuckie-boy!"* With a twist of its left arm and a mighty heave, the apparition hurled the gangster into the air.

Sol screamed shrilly as he flew through the darkened garage, tumbling over the hood and trunk of a pair of parked cars before crashing heavily against the wall behind them. Across the garage, the cloaked figure wheeled about in eerie slow motion and began to glide toward the moaning gangster.

Metal glinted in the shadows as the figure neared him, once again extending the curved blade at the end of its right arm. Sol huddled back against the wall, closing his eyes.

Suddenly tires screeched. The grinning death's head turned in the direction of the sound, the shadowy figure melting back into the darkness as a dark green roadster flashed around the far corner of the ramp on its way to the exit several floors below. As its taillights vanished around the next curve, the dark figure re-emerged from the shadows.

The gangster was gone. The skull mask lifted at the

faint sound of footsteps, scanning the garage with its dark eye sockets.

Several yards away, Chuckie Sol raced up the stairwell, his precious briefcase again tucked under one arm. His face was bruised, his collar bloody. He breathed in shallow gasps.

Sol mounted the top step and dashed out onto the roof lot. He paused to gaze up in relief at the stars shimmering in the hazy sky, then hurried on.

Unseen in the shadows behind him, a black-cloaked figure began to rise silently through the twisting stairwell, dark mist billowing beneath it.

Half a dozen cars were parked on the roof. Sol puffed to the side of an expensive-looking silver sports car. He fumbled his keys out of his jacket pocket and unlocked the driver's door. Heaving the battered case into the backseat, he slid behind the wheel. Sweat beaded his face. He slammed the door shut, jammed the key into the ignition, and jerked it to the right. The engine made a low, churning sound.

Across the garage, a pale death's head rose from the stairwell. The dark eye sockets surveyed the roof. The motor strained in the silver sports car as the cloaked figure glided toward it in a cloud of mist.

Sol was gnawing at his lower lip. As he gave the key its third turn, he glanced into the rearview mirror and saw the approaching figure. He made a strangled sound. Then the engine caught.

Sol gave a sob of relief. He snapped the headlights on, slipped the car into gear, and backed out of the parking place. With a grunt of triumph, he wheeled the car around and gunned the motor, speeding toward the dark apparition. When the front bumper was less than a yard away, the cloaked figure seemed to contract, mist coagulating around it. Then it leaped directly up into the air. A second later it landed on the hood of the sports car with a surprisingly substantial sound. Sol jerked back in surprise as the blade-wielding right arm drew back, then plunged forward into the windshield. Glass shattered inward. The gloved left hand reached for Chuckie Sol's throat through the jagged hole.

Before the clawing fingers could close on his flesh, Sol wrenched the steering wheel sharply to the left. The silver sports car swerved and the dark figure was hurled from the hood. Sol hit the gas pedal.

As he sped away, he shot a nervous glance into the rearview mirror. The apparition lay sprawled on the hard concrete floor, one arm twitching feebly above its body. Sol grinned fiercely. He slammed on the brakes, forcing the car into a tight U-turn. "Lousy, stinkin'—this time I got you," he rasped.

The car took off with a squeal of tires, heading directly toward the crumpled form. The figure struggled weakly to its feet as the car hurtled toward it. Black-clad arms appeared from beneath the ragged cloak and waved mystically in Sol's direction. A thick dark mist rose to completely envelop the figure. Sol hunched down behind the wheel, his teeth clenched in a fierce grin as he waited for the awful impact of steel crunching flesh and bones. The silver sports car plowed into the dark mist and out the other side.

"Huh?" The gangster craned his neck over his shoulder, scanning the rooftop behind him, his jaw

MASK OF THE PHANTASM

hanging in amazement. Black mist still clung to the car. Now it seemed to expand, pouring in through the shattered windshield and filling the interior of the speeding car.

"Wha-a-at?" Sol swiped at the air in front of his face, completely blinded. The mist cleared a bit and he leaned forward, trying to gauge his location. Several yards in front of the racing car stood a low retaining wall.

Beyond it was empty air.

THREE

Batman was racing along
the elevated bridge when he heard a muffled shout followed by the protracted screech of tires. He raised his
eyes to the rooftop parking lot just as the silver sports
car crashed through the concrete retaining wall and
sailed into the space above the walkway.

Moving with the speed of instinct, he drew his grappling gun from his cape and fired it toward an undam-
aged portion of the garage roof wall. He swung out
from the walkway as chunks of concrete rained down.
As he made a graceful arc toward the garage, the
sports car spiraled overhead and smashed nose-first
into the window of one of the Grand Imperator's
suites. It hung there, its horn blaring, embedded like a
silver thorn in the side of the hotel. Black smoke billowed from its back end, and shards of glass fell
toward the distant ground as the car's rear wheels spun
slowly to a stop.

Batman swung down to the ground. Expensively

MASK OF THE PHANTASM

dressed men and women had started to pour out of the casino. He stood unnoticed in the shadows at the base of the garage, and turned to look up at the smoking wreck. As he watched, the ruined car settled a foot deeper into the hole it had punched in the side of the building. The movement caused its back door to fall open. The latch of the battered briefcase had been sprung by the crash. Now flurries of counterfeit money began to drift down onto the gathering crowd below. The bystanders gazed up in awe, many of them moving swiftly to take advantage of the unexpected windfall.

"Hey!" A man in a tuxedo had appeared on a lower balcony of the hotel. He pointed down at the Dark Knight through the money storm. "Look—it's him!"

Eyes turned and other fingers began to point. Batman ignored the shouts and questions directed at him. As he turned to leave, a flicker of dark movement on the roof of the garage caught his attention.

A dark silhouette with a pale head was standing next to the ragged gap left in the retaining wall by Chuckie Sol's sports car. Batman stared at the apparition for a moment, then pulled out his grappling gun. Simultaneously, a cloud of thick black mist appeared out of nowhere to surround the motionless figure.

Batman narrowed his eyes at the garage. There appeared to be only one stairwell connecting the roof to the floor beneath it. He aimed the gun and fired upward. The grapple caught on an edge of the concrete wall. The Dark Knight pressed a stud on the gun and the slender line hauled him toward the roof with a faint humming sound. He swung into the level just below the roof and raced for the stairwell, confident that whoever he had glimpsed up above had not had time to use the steps. He stepped out onto the roof and scanned the area. There was no one there.

He raced to the parked cars and checked each one carefully. Nothing. He went to stand by the shattered wall, frowning thoughtfully as a wisp of dark vapor dissolved slowly into the night breeze. As he turned to leave, his black boot crunched on something lying on the concrete rooftop. He knelt to retrieve a two-inch fragment of clouded glass. Dropping the shard into a compartment of his utility belt, he straightened and headed back toward the stairwell.

FOUR

"I'm telling you, friends, it's vigilantism at its deadliest!"

Gotham City Councilman Arthur Reeves raised the forefinger of his right hand and looked squarely into the nearest television camera as he made his point. The crowd milling around the steps of City Hall murmured its approval as the handsome young politician paused for effect.

"He's playing them like a revivalist preacher," television reporter Summer Gleeson murmured to her cameraman on the sidelines. "He's slick, all right. Watch—now he'll go after Gordon."

"Commissioner Gordon," Reeves thundered, turning to the gray-haired man standing just behind him with a group of police officials, "I ask you. How many times are we going to let this happen?" Summer winced as the councilman's forefinger wagged inches beneath the older man's nose. "How many times are we going to let Batman cross the line?"

BATMAN: THE ANIMATED MOVIE

"Let's try to keep things in perspective, Councilman." James Gordon raised his hands placatingly. "We don't even know that a line's been crossed." Inwardly he was cursing the impulse that had made him agree to attend Reeves's impromptu press conference. He snorted. Press conference, indeed—the way Reeves ran things, it was more like a public indictment of Gordon and his methods. All that was missing was the tar and feathers.

"Excuse me?" Reeves blinked in surprise. "Do we not have the body of one Charlton Sol in residence at this very moment in the city morgue? If that—"

"I'm sorry, Councilman." Gordon raised his voice to cut through the rhetoric. "But you can't blame Batman for what happened to Chuckie Sol."

"What?" Reeves gaped at the crowd, inviting them to share his astonishment. "Why on earth not?" He snatched a newspaper from an aide and held it up to the battery of TV cameras. The front page headline proclaimed GANGSTER SLAIN above a photograph of Chuckie Sol's silver sports car embedded twelve stories up in the side of the Grand Imperator. "Numerous eyewitnesses have placed this self-styled crime fighter at the scene," Reeves continued. "He was there and he was after Sol. And now Sol is dead." The councilman lowered the newspaper with a doleful shake of his head. "He's a loose cannon, Commissioner."

Summer Gleeson repressed a sigh. She could see that Reeves was on the verge of working himself up into a fire-and-brimstone frenzy again. The man made some sense once in a great while—but he had too much flash and far too little substance for her to take

MASK OF THE PHANTASM

seriously. Watching the crowd's reaction to the councilman's charges, she had to admit that he was a world-class manipulator. Poor Gordon didn't stand a chance.

"It's not just my opinion," Reeves was saying in his most reasonable tone. "A lot of people—police officers included, I might add—have thought for quite some time that this Batman is every bit as unstable as the criminals he occasionally manages to apprehend." The councilman gestured toward his left, where Detective Harvey Bullock was trying vainly to hide his unshaven face behind the collar of his rumpled trench coat. Gordon glared meaningfully at his subordinate.

"Now I ask you, Commissioner—and I ask *you*, Gotham City"—Reeves brought his handsome face back to the camera—"just what kind of city are we running when we choose to depend on the support of a potential madman to enforce law and order?" The councilman paused for a breath, then—noticing that Gordon was moving toward the microphones with the intention of offering a rebuttal—he lifted his arms and leaned smoothly forward. "And that, concerned citizens and ladies and gentlemen of the press, is all that we have time for tonight. Thank you for coming and for your continued support—Gotham needs you!"

Summer shook her head, watching Gordon's expression change from dumbfounded to furious. He had a right to be upset, she reflected, scanning the crowd as they reacted to Reeves's final words. At least for the moment, the cheers outnumbered the boos by an easy ten to one.

* * *

"Such rot, sir."

Alfred Pennyworth shook his head in prim disapproval as Arthur Reeves's passionate features shrank to a pinpoint of bluish light on the large video screen, then vanished altogether. The butler set the remote control on a nearby outcropping of stone and turned to his employer. "Why, *I've* always found you to be the very model of sanity. Oh, by the way—" He paused to make a slight adjustment to the black-and-gray costume draped over his right arm. "I've polished the Batboat, pressed your tights, and put away your exploding gas pellets for the evening."

Bruce Wayne was hunched over a long laboratory table, poking at a fragment of discolored glass with a pair of tiny forceps. He brushed a lock of dark hair back from his forehead, a wry smile tugging briefly at his lips. "Thank you, Alfred."

The lab table sat in the center of a wide plateau of natural rock, one of many workstations occupying different levels in the vast cavern located beneath Wayne Manor. Lights placed strategically in the vaulted ceiling shone down on an array of highly sophisticated computers and an interlocking arrangement of laboratories furnished with state-of-the-art equipment, all designed to provide the best in crime-solving techniques. Ramps connected the workstations to a gallery of strange souvenirs—trophies from past cases—and an assortment of high-tech vehicles that provided unparalleled transportation capabilities in the air, on or beneath the water, and on the highway. In addition to the two men, the cavern was host to numerous other inhabitants, their presence signaled only by the faint,

MASH OF THE PHANTASM

ceaseless rustling of their leathery wings high above the workstations.

Alfred left the video monitor and crossed the plateau to peer over Bruce's shoulder. He raised a thin black eyebrow. "Might one inquire as to the object of your current investigation, Master Bruce?"

"It's a piece of safety glass I found at the scene of the accident." Bruce tugged at his chin, leaning back to regard the fragment thoughtfully. "Part of the late Chuckie Sol's windshield, if my hunch is correct." He reached out and pressed a small button on the console in front of him. To his right a rectangular section of metal flipped open. He placed the glass fragment into the shallow chamber and pushed the lid shut. With his left hand he tapped rapidly on a tiny keyboard.

A magnified image of the shard appeared on a monitor mounted above the lab table, the degree of amplification specified in blue numbers in the lower right-hand corner of the screen. Other information was given in green on the left. "See there?" The numbers and letters changed rapidly as Bruce's hand played over the keyboard. "There's a chemical residue baked onto it, as I suspected—some kind of dense, long-chain polymer."

"Ah." Alfred raised the other brow. "I should have known." He turned with a minuscule shrug and moved toward the cylindrical elevator that connected the Batcave to the mansion above. "Dinner will be served in precisely one hour, Master Bruce," he announced over his shoulder as the door slid open. "Do try to tear yourself away from your dense chains before the vichyssoise grows too warm."

FIVE

Burton Earny did not like to work, and that was about all there was to it. This was less a result of any inherent laziness, Burt believed, than the fallout from a long series of ill-suited placements in the vocational world. His first job, acquired after much protest when he was seventeen, had been at a combination coin-op laundry and soft-serve ice cream parlor down the block from his parents' home in the sleepy surburban community of Perry Village. The Frostee Fluff occupied two halves of a modest one-story brick building. A big plywood ice cream cone sat on the shingled roof above the soft-serve half, while something that was intended to be a laundry basket piled high with soiled clothing adorned the other side. The company that manufactured the ingredients for the soft serve had supplied the ice cream cone, but the laundry basket had been designed and executed by the wife of the Frostee Fluff's owner, and most customers told Burt that they took it to be a representation of a rather unappetizing hot fudge sundae.

Burt was almost always miserable on the days that he worked at the Frostee Fluff, but he particularly disliked Sunday afternoons between 1 and 5 and Thursday mornings from 8 till noon. Those were the hours that the owner, Mr. Fred Datwillig, chose to spend in the bosom of his small family, leaving Burt alone to handle both sides of the enterprise.

A single doorway connected the soft serve shop with the laundry, and a small silver servants' bell sat attached by a string to a counter on each side. Burt quickly grew to detest the sound of those bells. Years later, certain noises still gave him goose bumps—the ringing of those little metal devices that were sometimes mounted on bicycle handlebars being the worst. Until he was in his mid-twenties, he would wake up about twice a year in a cold sweat from a nightmare in which he was standing at the exact center of the connecting doorway of the Frostee Fluff, trying to dole out Chocolate Mountains and Banana Buddies to hyperactive children with his left hand, while simultaneously keeping an army of little old ladies supplied with dryer change with his right. When his breathing had calmed, Burt would inevitably find that his alarm clock had been ringing for the past half hour, and that he was now going to lose another job due to chronic tardiness.

In the years following his stint at the Frostee Fluff, Burt had tried his hand at a variety of vocations. From parrot wrangler at the Perry Village Pet Parlor to fry cook at the Greenfeed Health Food Café, his attempts at finding gainful employment of a rewarding nature had met uniformly with failure.

During the summer of his twenty-eighth year, Burt and his mother and father had joined thousands of others in making the two-hour pilgrimage to the big city to attend the Gotham World's Fair. While there, Burt had been coaxed by his parents to sign up for a battery of aptitude tests offered by a corporation that used computers to assess one's likelihood of finding employment. The skills analysis was disappointingly inconclusive, while the examination of likes and dislikes revealed that Burt—who had only once ventured farther from Perry Village than the mall located two exits down on the interstate—craved the experience of *travel* more than anything else in the world. Unfortunately, one needed money to travel and a job to make money, and Burt hated to work.

Two days after his thirty-seventh birthday, Burt Earny had left the quiet neighborhood where he had been born and headed off with a new necktie, an old suitcase, and a bus ticket to seek his fortune elsewhere. Burt had purchased the necktie himself. The suitcase and the bus ticket were provided by his parents who, while they loved their son dearly, had been planning for several years to convert his old bedroom into a showplace for Mr. Earny's kaleidoscope collection and his wife's macramé animals. Two days and three hours after his birthday, Burt had disembarked at the Gotham Bus Terminal, suitcase in hand.

Surprisingly, the employment situation was not much better in the big city than it had been in the

MASH OF THE PHANTASM

small town. Burt had already gone through three jobs (fruit waxer, fish scaler, and washroom attendant) by the time he applied for work as a chip buffer at the Shady Lady.

The Grand Imperator Hotel had recently embarked on a campaign designed to attract a more upscale clientele to its casino, and the consultant they had engaged to choreograph their upward movement had suggested that someone be hired to sit in a ground-floor window and polish betting chips of various denominations with a chamois cloth.

Burt felt the interview had gone well, though he had choked a bit when the discussion wandered to "previous buffing experience." Luckily he had remembered an uncle who had shown an almost pathological fondness for polishing his old Ford pickup in the Earnys' driveway every other afternoon, and Burt had been able to draw upon his observations of his uncle's technique when framing his response.

At the end of the interview, Burt left the casino and made his way down the short corridor that connected the Shady Lady with the hotel lobby. Strolling to the bank of gleaming elevators, he stepped into a waiting car and punched the button for the top floor. Apparently the highest floor was reserved for those wealthy enough to afford the penthouse suite—and access to a private elevator—for the car deposited him instead on the floor beneath. Unperturbed, Burt sauntered down the corridor to the red exit sign, pushed open the heavy metal door, and accomplished the remaining flight under his own steam. He emerged red-faced and puffing from the stairwell and went straight to a large

BATMAN: THE ANIMATED MOVIE

window at the end of the carpeted hallway. He stepped up to the windowsill with his eyes closed, took a deep breath, and looked out.

Gotham City was spread out before him in all its spangled glory. Lights winked on and off at the tops of nearby skyscrapers, blazed in executive office towers occupied at this late hour by regiments of custodial engineers, and wove red and white streamers in complicated traffic patterns beneath him. Burt dusted off a small area of the windowsill with his sleeve and set down the rumpled brown paper bag that he felt obliged to carry tucked under his right arm any time he left his tiny rented room to go forth into the city. The bag contained a camera, a birthday gift from his mother and father, given to him on the condition that he use it in another town—preferably one outside a fifty-mile radius of Perry Village.

Burt made sure the bag was safe, leaned his elbows on the sill, and rested his round chin in his palms. He looked out over the sparkling immensity that was Gotham and gave a contented sigh.

Then he noticed the man with the briefcase.

A parking garage was attached to the Grand Imperator by concrete walkways on several different levels. The topmost walkway extended from the penthouse floor, accessed through a door at the other end of the corridor from the window where Burt now stood. A sudden flash of motion in the corner of his eye caught his attention, and he craned his neck to watch as a middle-aged man with a brown briefcase came jogging along just inside the outer wall of the garage on the same level as Burt. The man kept looking back over his shoulder.

From the unkempt appearance of his clothes and hair, Burt guessed that the man had been involved in a mugging, or at least a serious disagreement with a larger individual. The man reached the stairwell and clambered up toward the garage roof with a panicky look on his pale face. Then he was gone. The angle of the window made it impossible to see anything that was happening above the low retaining wall that bordered the rooftop of the garage. Burt was about to look away when something drew his eyes back to the stairs.

A shadowy figure was moving slowly up through the stairwell, which suddenly seemed to be filling with clouds of murky smoke. Exhaust fumes? It seemed too thick and dark for that. Burt bit his lower lip, torn between the desire to continue his observation of this strange drama, and the realization that he should probably be looking for a way to summon the proper authorities about now. Police? Fire department? He hovered anxiously at the window as the dark figure reached the top of the steps and disappeared from view.

He scanned the near side of the roof, looking for some sign of either of the two who had ascended the stairs. When he dropped his eyes to the stairwell again, he was startled to see that the dark clouds had almost completely dissipated, only a few stray wisps left swirling by the railing. So much for the fire department. And what could he tell the police that would justify sending out a patrol car? Burt shrugged and gave the rooftop a last inspection, then turned back to the dazzling cityscape.

He reached into the paper bag and drew out his camera. With the special film he had purchased, he thought he should be able to get several decent pictures of nighttime Gotham. The camera store also carried do-it-yourself postcards with adhesive backs, and he had bought a package of six with yesterday's snack money. Burt grinned. Wouldn't his parents be surprised when they received a homemade Gotham City postcard from their inventive son! Burt raised the lens to his eye and began to choose his subject.

It was about that time that the silver sports car dived off the roof of the garage and spiraled down into the side of the Grand Imperator.

Burt found the experience very reminiscent of the action movies that were so popular nowadays. He had swung his head around when he heard the initial impact of steel on concrete as the car burst through the retaining wall, and from then on everything seemed to happen in slow motion. He noticed that one of the sports car's retractable headlights had been damaged by the drive through the wall. He saw the cloud of swirling mist clinging to the sports car's windshield. He got a close enough look through the driver's window to identify the driver as the man with the briefcase. Then the car struck the hotel with a resounding crash and everything trembled for a few seconds. As he lowered his hands from his face, Burt's finger tightened reflexively on the shutter button and the camera

MASH OF THE PHANTASM

went off with a click and a whirr, wasting the first shot on a very expensive roll of film.

Burt grimaced and gave the camera a shake, as if to reprimand it. Then he had an idea.

The TV was filled with those eyewitness, I-was-there video programs, and Burt was positive the producers paid big bucks to anyone lucky enough to find themselves and their video camera on the scene at a really big disaster. Burt had never owned a video camera, but he did have almost an entire roll of expensive film and a unique vantage point. Maybe the newspapers would be willing to make a trade: a few award-winning photos of a car embedded in the side of a hotel in exchange for enough cash to get him on a tramp steamer bound for the south seas.

He frowned, not entirely certain tramp steamers still existed—or if they did, exactly who was living in the south seas, and if they still welcomed tourists. He gave a mental shrug and aimed the camera down at the smoking wreck. He would be more than happy to settle for a six-day cruise to the Caribbean.

Burt used up most of the roll, hurried down the stairs to the floor below, and headed for the elevator.

The silver sports car had apparently caused some damage to one of the hotel's electrical cables, for the lights went out and the elevator car lurched to a stop halfway between the sixth and fifth floors, leaving Burt to cool his heels for a long ten minutes before finally disgorging him into the thronging lobby.

It was not until the next day, when Burt scanned a seatmate's morning newspaper on the subway, that he

learned about the squall of counterfeit money that had
fallen from Chuckie Sol's car while he loitered between floors—and of the dramatic appearance of the
individual most people were calling responsible for
the murder of the man with the briefcase: Batman.

SIX

Clouds raced and roiled around the body of the sleek passenger plane. Below, the sprawl of miniature buildings caught in a baffling web of thread-sized highways had begun to grow into an imposing cityscape as the airplane started its slow approach to the Gotham City Airport.

"We should be touching down any minute now." Andrea Beaumont sat forward in her first-class seat and gazed out the small window as she spoke softly into a portable phone. She was a strikingly attractive, smartly dressed woman in her late twenties, with compelling blue-green eyes and chestnut hair arranged in the latest style. An antique gold locket hung on a chain about her slender neck. "It'll be good to see you again, Arthur."

"You, too," came the voice from the phone. Andrea imagined Councilman Arthur Reeves sitting back in a black leather chair in his tastefully furnished city office. Knowing Arthur, he was probably checking his appearance in a pocket mirror while they spoke. "Don't worry about a thing," Reeves told her in carefully modulated tones. "We'll clear up these old family finances in no time. Don't forget—you've got a big-time city councilman on your side."

"I appreciate that, Arthur." Andrea tilted her head, gazing raptly down at the city swelling darkly beneath her. "Gotham," she murmured, her thoughts beginning to wander. "I can't believe it's been ten years. . . ."

"So. Thinking of looking up some old friends?" Reeves prompted after several moments of silence. The heartiness in his voice sounded forced.

Andrea frowned, glancing down almost guiltily at the copy of *Success* magazine resting on her lap. The cover sported a portrait of a ruggedly handsome, dark-haired man, under a banner that announced PROFILE: BRUCE WAYNE.

Andrea touched the picture gently with the tips of her fingers. "Oh, Arthur," she said into the phone, "don't start that again. He's ancient history."

"That's encouraging," Reeves said. "Then I'll see you soon—and happy landing."

Andrea lowered the phone and sat looking at the glossy picture. She raised her head with a start when a flight attendant appeared at the front of the cabin.

"Ladies and gentlemen," the young man said, including Andrea in his professional smile. "Please fasten your seat belts. We're beginning our descent into Gotham City."

MASK OF THE PHANTASM

Andrea checked her seat belt obediently. She started to slide the magazine into her bag, hesitated, and slipped it into the pocket of the seat in front of her instead. Then she turned back to the window and watched as the great city rose to meet her.

SEVEN

Outside the huge structure, rain fell steadily on the dozens of expensive automobiles that lined the great circular driveway of Wayne Manor. Inside, an entire room had been set aside for the guests' umbrellas. Alfred added a large model with alternating white and maroon panels to the collection and returned to the main hall.

The mansion echoed with the sounds of laughter and soft music. Moving carefully under Alfred's watchful eye, half a dozen waiters carried trays laden with pale champagne and colorful delicacies along their assigned routes from one side of the hall to the other. The butler surveyed the nearby guests, noting the usual mixture of politicians, media personalities, and wealthy entrepreneurs. Like every other aspect of Master Bruce's life, Alfred reflected, the young billionaire's parties were masterpieces of artfully disguised calculation. He scanned the room, his lips quirking ironically when he spotted his employer. He watched for a few moments, then turned with a barely perceptible shake of his head and went to straighten the collar of one of the waiters.

Bruce stood at the heart of the great hall, at the center of his guests' attention in the middle of a trio of beautiful women.

The three seemed to be involved in a contest to see which could stand closest to their wealthy host.

"Come on, Bruce," said the tanned blonde on his left, pressing her hip against his as she reached up to brush an imaginary eyelash from his cheek. "All alone in this big mansion, with rooms for days and all these toys. Haven't you ever thought about marriage—not even once?"

The ebony-skinned woman on his immediate right went up on tiptoe to place her hands playfully over his ears. "Oh, never say the *M* word in front of Bruce, darling," she cooed. "It makes him nervous."

The third beauty was pale, with short red hair. She surveyed the scene with a tiny frown, as if trying to figure out a route past her competition and into their host's arms. "What about the *I* word, then?" she inquired innocently.

Bruce turned to regard her quizzically, his attention snared. "The *I* word?" he asked.

"You know"—she batted her long lashes—"engagement."

Bruce gave his crooked half smile as the nearby onlookers reacted with glee. Bachelorette number three was preparing to pursue her advantage with a frontal attack, when a sharp elbow caught her in the ribs. A fourth woman, dressed in a revealing black gown,

BATMAN: THE ANIMATED MOVIE

stepped past her to smile up at Bruce. She was also beautiful, her skin the color of old ivory and her long straight hair as black as a raven's wing. She smiled sardonically as she tipped her drink at their host.

"I'd watch out for Brucie if I were you, girls." Her voice had the first traces of an alcohol-induced slur. "First he wines and dines you," she went on, fixing Bruce with a wavering stare. "Makes you think you're the only woman he's ever been interested in. And just when you're wondering where to register the china pattern—" She paused dramatically, her lips drawing back from perfect white teeth. "—He forgets your phone number."

Bruce was watching the proceedings with a casual detachment. It wasn't the first time one too many trips to an open bar had caused this kind of confrontation with one of the women he had briefly dated. He waited with an air of faint amusement for the woman to run out of steam.

Then a look of sudden fury appeared on her carefully decorated features and she hauled her slim arm back and threw her drink in his face.

There was a mutual gasp as his trio of admirers drew back in horror. The black-haired woman gave her head a short, sharp nod and stalked off in the direction of the bar.

Bruce stood stock-still. Then he lifted his hand and wiped his eyes with his fingers, stone-faced.

"Excuse me," he said with a small bow to the three women. He turned on his heel and strode off.

"A friend in need?"

Bruce recognized the suave tones before he saw the

face. Then Arthur Reeves appeared at his side, dangling a linen handkerchief in front of the other man's face. Bruce took the square of cloth and swabbed at his eyes and cheeks.

"Councilman," he said with a nod. "So how goes the bat bashing?"

"Better than your love life, apparently." Reeves raised his brows toward the scene of Bruce's recent dampening. "Really, old man, it's almost as if you pick them deliberately because you know there's absolutely no chance for a serious relationship." Alfred hove into view bearing a tray of champagne flutes. The councilman plucked one from the tray as it passed by, earning himself a sideward glance of disapproval from the proper butler. "Although there was that one girl . . . Oh, let me see—" He screwed his face up in an expression of exaggerated concentration. "What *was* her name?"

Bruce had been dabbing at his collar with the handkerchief. He stood frozen as Reeves continued his game.

"Hmmm," the councilman mused. "Was it Anne . . . Andi . . . *Andrea!*" He smiled lazily at Bruce. "That was it. Andrea Beaumont. Now *there* was a sweet number. How'd you let that one fall out of your address book?"

Bruce carefully folded the stained handkerchief, his eyes on the floor. "Thanks for the use of the rag, Arthur," he said in a low, controlled voice. "You know where you can stick it." He reached out and stuffed the damp cloth deep into Reeves's breast pocket, turned, and stalked off.

Alfred glided by again as Reeves stood staring after his host. "You may wish to freshen up, Councilman," the butler said with a nod at the twisted end of hand-kerchief protruding from the other man's pocket. "Your clothing seems to have become a bit disar-rayed."

EIGHT

Bruce entered his study and closed the door behind him, a dark expression on his face. Rain fell in sheets against the window and lightning tore the sky. He stood at his desk and toyed with a paperweight made from a fossilized ammonite, his eyes on the portrait of his late parents that hung above the crackling fireplace.

The faces in the picture seemed stern and unsmiling this evening, with an aura of Victorian propriety. Bruce crossed slowly to the fireplace and leaned his arm on the mantle, staring down into the fire. Images seemed to dance and flicker in the leaping flames as his thoughts drifted back to a day ten years past.

It was late autumn. Brown and gold leaves blew through the cemetery with a faint clattering sound. A youthful Bruce stood with his arm resting on the marble monument that marked his parents' grave. The wind had pushed his collar askew and his dark hair was disheveled. He held two long-stemmed roses in his hand. He knelt solemnly to lay them on the manicured grass in front of the headstone. Then he got to his feet and stood with his hands thrust into the pockets of his overcoat, a brooding expression on his face.

"That's right. And if Daddy gets any more protective, I might as well join the Young Republicans. . . ."

Bruce lifted his head in surprise and craned his neck toward the sound of the voice. A young woman was standing among a group of headstones not far from the Wayne monument. She gestured with her arms and made a comment Bruce could not hear. From his vantage point, she appeared to be standing by herself. Puzzled, he moved closer.

"It's times like this I wish you were around to . . ." Her voice dipped out of range again as the breeze lifted her light brown hair into a flowing nimbus about her profile. She was reaching up a hand to smooth it back when Bruce's shadow crept into view on the ground beside her. She wheeled around to face him. "Yes?"

"Uh. Excuse me." Bruce felt his cheeks redden under her stare. "I thought you were saying something. To me, I mean."

Andrea raised her eyes as if gauging the distance between her location and the Wayne monument. "No," she said shortly and turned her back.

"Oh," Bruce stood for an awkward moment, looking at the graceful lines of her back. As far as he could see, there was no one else in the immediate vicinity. "O-kay," he said slowly. He turned and walked away.

"Know who that was?" The brown-haired woman

looked down at her feet. Her voice sounded excited. "That was Bruce Wayne. You know—Wayne Enterprises? I've seen him on campus. Very moody. Cute, though—don't you think?"

Bruce was several yards away by this time. He stopped and shook his head, then turned back with a sigh.

The young woman looked back over her shoulder at the sound, her eyebrows lifted in polite inquiry. "Yes?"

Bruce glanced to right and left, satisfying himself that there was indeed no one else in the area. "I heard my name mentioned," he began. "I thought . . ." He exhaled with a shrug. "Look—*who* are you talking to?"

The young woman brushed a wisp of hair back from her cheek and gestured to the ground in front of her. "My mother." For the first time Bruce noticed the simple stone marker laid flush with the grass.

IN LOVING MEMORY

VICTORIA BEAUMONT

"Oh," Bruce flushed with embarrassment, looking from the grave marker to the bright-eyed young woman. "I'm sorry. I didn't mean to . . ."

"That's okay. We're done." She picked up her bag and patted his arm. "Mom doesn't have much to say today." She caught his sidelong glance as she walked by. "Hey, I'm not the only one who talks to their loved ones, you know," she said defensively. She slung the strap of her bag over her shoulder and headed for the path.

"I didn't say anything," Bruce called after her. He hesitated for a moment, then turned to follow. He caught up to her and they continued side by side down the path toward the cemetery gate.

"It's just that when I talk to her out loud, it's easier to imagine how she'd reply," Andrea said as they walked. "Like she's right there." She shrugged. "It makes a difference, somehow."

Bruce nodded thoughtfully. "I talked to my parents after they died," he said. "Once."

"What did you say?"

He ushered her through the big wrought-iron gate. "I made a vow."

She raised her eyebrows. "What vow?"

"A secret one." His tone had become a bit distant.

"Oooh—a man of mystery!" She turned to study his face, her hands clasped at her breast in mock fascination. "And have you kept your vow?"

His expression stayed sober. "So far."

They had reached the street outside the cemetery. A sleek convertible was parked at the curb in front of Bruce's staid roadster. Andrea walked over to the car and dropped her bag onto the passenger seat. Then she turned and walked back to Bruce.

"Andrea Beaumont." She extended her hand in a formal gesture.

They shook. "Bruce Wayne."

MASK OF THE PHANTASM

"I know." She gave a wry smile. " 'Boy billionaire.' So tell me, Bruce"—she reached up to straighten his collar—"with all that money and power, how come you always look like you want to jump off the nearest cliff?"

Bruce smiled in spite of himself. He gave his head a small shake as he followed her back to the convertible. "Why should you care about that?"

"Oh, I don't." She slid into the driver's seat and turned the key. The car purred to life. Andrea smiled cheerfully. "Mother was just wondering." She put the car in gear and pulled away from the curb.

Bruce stood watching her, a bemused smile on his face. The autumn breeze was turning brisk and leaves rustled at his feet as the sun drifted behind a bank of high clouds.

NINE

In the study, Bruce raised his head, his thoughts called back to the present by a burst of laughter from the main hall. Reluctant to rejoin his guests, he lifted a poker and jabbed idly at the log in the fireplace. His mind wandered back to the past again as the flames leaped in response. . . .

The moon looked like it belonged in an amateur oil painting, too full and bright to have a place in the real world. The wind whistled as a trio of black bats flitted beneath its glowing orb. Wisps of cloud raced across its face in a ragged veil.

It was late. Gotham Mall had closed its doors to window-shoppers and customers alike hours earlier. Now the stores stood silent, their clever facades making them resemble a row of abandoned playthings.

A figure clothed in form-fitting black swung into the pale circle of light cast by the nearest streetlight. He released the end of his slender rope and dropped

MASK OF THE PHANTASM

somewhat awkwardly onto the roof of the mall. The intruder skirted around the huge fedora advertising Big Hat men's clothiers, ducked past the enormous bouquet of Everbloom's Floral Shoppe, and raced under the smirking clown face propped above the Lucky Chuckles Arcade.

He paused to catch his breath, the moonlight silvering his features as he peered around the edge of a smoking chimney stack. Bruce Wayne had traded his overcoat for a black turtleneck and a pair of black jeans. Around his waist was a wide leather belt to which had been fastened a second length of rope and half a dozen makeshift pouches. A black wool cap was pulled low on his forehead. He looked around to make sure no one had spotted him, ducked back into the shadows, and moved on.

A muffled crashing sound came from the other side of the building. Bruce sprinted to the edge of the roof and looked down.

Four stories below, a semitrailer had been backed down a long narrow alleyway up to one of the mall loading docks. Bruce squinted and made out two burly men in the dim light. One of them was looking down at a smashed VCR, apparently the topmost of the armload he had been carrying from the door to the truck. His partner, a short man whose arms were laden with boxes of jewelry and watches, stepped up to him.

"Hey, dummy—what's a matter wit' choo? Dis is expensive merchandise." The shorter crook made no attempt to keep his voice down. Kicking the wrecked machine out of his way, he continued on toward the van. The first man followed with a scowl.

BATMAN: THE ANIMATED MOVIE

Bruce moved to a better vantage point on the rooftop and gazed down on the scene. Just inside the loading dock, a night guard was tied up on the ground, watching helplessly. As the second crook disappeared into the van of the truck, the guard began to struggle against the ropes.

"Comin' through." A third burglar emerged from the warehouse, a pair of heavy, marble-based table lamps under his arms. He nodded politely to the guard, stepping over the recumbent form on his way to the truck. The guard cringed.

Bruce surveyed the scene anxiously. After two long minutes passed with no new players, he decided that the three hoodlums he had seen so far constituted the entire gang. He took a deep breath. Then he reached up and unrolled the wool cap into a black ski mask that covered his face with holes for his eyes and mouth. "Here goes," he murmured to himself, detaching the loop of rope from his belt.

The third burglar secured the lamps at the rear of the truck, as the short crook pulled a cheap walkie-talkie from his belt. "Okay, Skaz," he said. "The boys 'n' me're done shoppin'."

At the far end of the alley another man stepped out of the shadows and waved his arms to his confederate. He was wearing a cap secured with a tie-dyed bandanna. Underneath the colorful scarf was a microphone and headset. He glanced right and left and brought the mike to his lips. The walkie-talkie crackled. "All clear here."

The short man jammed the antenna into the top of the walkie-talkie and snapped it back on his belt. He walked to the back of the truck and swung the doors shut. "Okay, gents," he growled. "Let's blow this clambake!"

A bloodcurdling cry split the silence, and all three hoods turned to gape upward as a black-clad figure dropped out of the night to land with a loud thud on the roof of the semi. There was a moment's silence, then the sound of rapid footsteps.

The intruder suddenly appeared again. Arms and legs pumping, he hurtled headlong off the end of the truck. He tucked his body into a series of graceful somersaults, twisted in midair, and landed on the edge of the loading dock facing the astonished crooks. Bruce wobbled slightly, then regained his balance, straightening into a classic martial arts stance. Behind him in the warehouse entranceway, the security guard's eyes bulged above the cloth gag.

"All right," Bruce said in his most menacing tones. His voice sounded nervous and unsure to him, like a teenager pretending to be a drill sergeant. "Flat on your stomachs," he barked, "Arms spread—*now!*"

The three men at the truck looked at the intruder and then at each other. "Who *is* dis clown?" snarled the short man. He looked past Bruce at the trussed-up guard. "Hey, sis—you know dis guy?"

The guard shook her head.

"You heard me!" Bruce said, his voice faltering slightly. He raised his fist and took a threatening step forward.

"Oh, yeah—" The short burglar looked apologetic. "We're really sorry about the delay." He motioned to his two confederates. "C'mon, boys. You heard Mr.

Kung Fu.'' Bruce glanced from left to right as the other two crooks moved out a few paces to either side.

''Yeah, we're shakin','' said the hood on the left. He and his partner each took another step, then another, putting Bruce in the center of a tight triangle on the narrow loading dock. The short crook took a step backward and picked up a crowbar from the dock near the truck. He slapped it into his palm with a nasty grin.

''Now!'' he said. The other two whipped guns out of their pockets and advanced toward the unarmed man.

Bruce stood his ground, his hand unsnapping one of the pouches affixed to his belt. He pulled out a pair of gleaming metal circles with points studding their rims. As the crooks charged him, he spun around, sending a ninja star flying toward each of the hoods.

The heavyset burglar on the left gave a yelp of pain as the sharp-pointed weapon struck his gun hand. The pistol went spinning off the loading dock onto the pavement. The second star hit the arm of the crook on the right. ''Ow! Jeez!'' His gun discharged harmlessly onto the ground as he jerked his arm back toward his body. He dropped the pistol, clutching his wounded arm in his other hand with a hoarse cry.

The short man's jaw hung open in disbelief. ''Get 'im!'' he shouted, raising the crowbar over his head and lunging toward Bruce with a ragged battle cry. The black-clad figure crouched, wheeled in a half circle, and kicked the hoodlum in the groin. The short man's battle cry became a shriek of pain. As his adversary doubled over in shock, Bruce reached out and grabbed the hem of his jacket, pulled it over his head, then brought his knee up to smash the crook's face. The short man tumbled backward.

The burglar on the left had circled behind Bruce. Now he raced in and grabbed him in a headlock as his partner ran up from the front. As Bruce struggled with the big man at his back, the second burglar delivered a roundhouse punch to Bruce's belly, knocking the wind out of him. The man who held him hauled Bruce's head up, his massive arm cutting off Bruce's air as the other crook slammed his fist into his face. Bruce grunted and fell limp in the hulking crook's arms.

"Aww, I think our little ka-rah-tay kid's had enough," the big man cooed. Just then Bruce thrust his head back, slamming into the burglar's forehead with the back of his skull. There was an awful cracking sound and the crook lurched backward, stunned. Bruce ducked through the big man's arms just as the last thug wound up for a knockout punch. The punch struck the big crook, who keeled over like a felled oak.

Snikkkt. The remaining thug brandished a six-inch switchblade. Bruce feinted back as the enraged man began slashing the air between them. One slash cut Bruce's sweater open at the level of his stomach. The crook narrowed his eyes triumphantly. On the next thrust, Bruce's hand struck the knife arm like a cobra, his fingers clamping hard on the other man's wrist. Bruce drew his leg up and delivered a pair of savage kicks just beneath the hood's armpit. Pirouetting like a dancer, Bruce swung his heel into the crook's esophagus, sending him flying into a trio of garbage cans lined up against the wall just to the right of the night guard. The bound woman stared, struggling to sit upright as the body struck the cans and dropped to the floor of the dock, out cold.

Bruce stood with feet spread wide, hands poised in the air at his sides, ready for the next assault. Only his rapid breathing betrayed the exertion of the last few minutes. He looked from one unconscious body to the next, excitement growing inside. "Yes!" he exulted, slamming his fist into his palm. He heard an urgent-sounding mumble and looked to where the security guard had managed to struggle to her feet against the loading dock entranceway. She gestured desperately with her head, trying to draw his attention to the other end of the alley.

The first shot whizzed past him as he turned to look down the side of the long truck. Bruce leaped to one side and somersaulted along the loading dock as the man called Skaz peppered the dock with gunfire. As he fired, Skaz climbed up to the cab of the semi and pulled the door open. Bruce lunged for the nearest garbage can and held it in front of his body like a shield. A bullet struck the metal with a loud *ping*. He dropped the can and somersaulted toward the entrance to the building, grabbing the helpless guard when he reached the doorway and pulling her inside with him. The shooting stopped a few seconds later. Bruce heard the cab door slam shut and the truck's motor rev. He was lying half sprawled across the guard's supine body. He got to his feet and gave her an apologetic nod. "Excuse me," he said politely.

MASK OF THE PHANTASM

In the cab, Skaz slipped the clutch into first and gunned the motor.

Bruce dashed back onto the dock just as the truck lurched forward. At its rear, the unlocked doors swung open and loose boxes and appliances began to spill out into the alleyway. Bruce leaped down from the loading dock, twisting his leg slightly as he landed on the slick cylinder of one of the marble lamps. The guard craned her neck around the edge of the doorway to watch in wonder as the man in black took off at a limping run after the accelerating truck.

A pair of speed bumps was evenly spaced along the alley. A minor avalanche occurred as the truck hit each bump, and a steady stream of stolen items tumbled out onto the pavement.

Bruce pounded down the alleyway, gradually catching up to the truck as he dodged microwaves and leaped over VCRs. He had almost reached the rear doors when the truck barreled out of the alleyway and started across the mall's parking lot.

Skaz put the engine into high gear and jammed his foot down on the gas pedal. Bruce took a deep breath and made a flying leap after the retreating truck. The left-hand door was swinging toward him. He tried to grab its handle as body and door came together, but the impact knocked his hand aside. He dropped just short of the truck, his fingers closing on the bottom of the door at the last instant.

He hung on desperately as the truck trundled across the empty lot, his boots sliding and skipping along the pavement. He finally found a better grip and strained to pull himself up and into the back of the truck.

There was a heavy-duty hammer lying on the floor of the truck just inside the door. Bruce bent to retrieve it, jamming it into the rear of his belt. The huge vehicle swung out onto the main road just then, dislodging a box of jewelry that opened as it fell toward him. He deflected the box with his arm, grimacing as necklaces and bracelets draped themselves momentarily over his ski mask. Pulling himself deeper into the van, he saw that nearly half its contents had already fallen out. What remained were mainly heavy-duty items, including a combination washer-dryer and a couple of mammoth refrigerators. Bruce inspected them with concern. The rope that bound them to the sides of the van looked none too sturdy. He turned to peer out the back of the vehicle, trying to get his bearings.

The semi swerved over a low curb as Skaz headed toward a highway entrance ramp. As the truck lurched onto the incline, the rope holding the refrigerators snapped neatly in two.

Bruce heard a rumbling noise at his back. He turned to see the pair of huge refrigerators sliding toward him. He dodged frantically. One of the massive appliances struck his side as they hurtled out the door, knocking him over the edge of the van.

He thrust out his hand, his fingers closing on the handle of the left-hand door as he lost his footing. He swung out to the side as the appliances crashed onto the ramp behind the truck.

The semi picked up speed on the flat road, rushing like a juggernaut into the heart of Gotham.

TEN

Officer Raymond T. O'Neil was nearing the end of his worst day in a week filled with lousy days. If life could just once go the way he wanted it to, he thought, he'd be home this very minute eating corned beef and cabbage with his wife, Eileen, and their twins, Troy and Mary.

As he drove the police cruiser along the wide boulevard in Gotham's midtown, O'Neil glared over at the source of his recent misery: his new partner, one Harvey T. Bullock by name.

Bullock was a thoroughly obnoxious man and a slovenly one to boot, whose uniform seemed to spontaneously break out in stains short minutes after he put it on each day. As O'Neil watched, Bullock was in the process of washing down the last of the three doughnuts he had managed to consume since the two men began their beat. How Bullock was able to eat and drink—and belch—continuously, all without ever removing the wooden toothpick he kept clamped in the corner of his mouth, was beyond O'Neil's ability to comprehend. He snorted with disgust and returned his gaze to the road.

A large semitrailer had begun to pull up alongside them on the right. Officer Bullock glanced idly over as the truck went by. The rear doors of the truck's van were swinging loose, he noticed. Definitely worth a citation. Bullock took another swallow of coffee and looked again. Hanging onto the nearest door, his legs dangling above the street, was a black-clad man in a black ski mask.

Interesting way to travel, Bullock thought, lifting his Styrofoam cup. Then the realization of what he had just seen sank in, and the next moment, the thick-set officer was spitting half a cup of coffee and one soggy toothpick onto the windshield in front of him.

Raymond T. O'Neil grimaced in fury as he watched the brown stream splatter against the glass. O'Neil had had all that he could take of his partner's filthy habits. As he prepared to reprimand the younger man in the sternest terms possible, Bullock pointed to the rear of the passing truck. "There's a guy out there in a black mask," the big man stammered, "swingin' back and forth like a lantern on a caboose!"

"Wha-a-at!" After twisting his neck for a corroborating glance, O'Neil turned on the flashing lights and punched the siren. Then he floored the gas and took off after the truck and its unusual passenger.

Officer Bullock reached inside his uniform and stuck a new toothpick in the corner of his mouth.

MASK OF THE PHANTASM

Grinning at his partner, he tightened his seat belt around his ample waist and leaned back in anticipation. He'd only just transferred to this precinct, and he'd expected to have to wait a while before his first car chase. This must be his lucky day!

ELEVEN

The crook called Skaz had checked his rearview mirror as soon as he heard the siren start. He saw the approaching police car with its red and blue lights spinning and wondered who they were after. He bit his lower lip as they swung into the lane behind him, hoping there was nothing wrong with the truck's headlights that could cause the cops to stop him. Then the lefthand rear door swung out into view and Skaz saw the masked man hanging on for dear life from its handle. He swore as he realized what had gotten the cops so agitated. Then he floored the gas pedal. There was no way he could let them stop him now.

The cops were coming up fast on his left side. Skaz gave the steering wheel a sudden turn. The truck veered sharply into the left lane in front of the police car.

He looked up ahead and got an idea. He yanked the wheel again. The truck swerved and suddenly there was a jarring impact. Skaz laughed. He had maneuvered the truck to smash the swinging back door into a lamppost. His unwanted passenger held on desperately. A few more of those, Skaz thought, and he'd be rid of half his problem, anyway.

The police car had fallen back and moved into the right lane. It increased speed, gaining slowly on the swerving truck. Skaz looked back and forth, dividing his attention between the man swinging from the door in his left rearview mirror and the cop car starting to pass him in his right. He eased up slightly on the gas, scowling menacingly as the police car nosed ahead and slid into the lane in front of him.

He jammed his foot down hard on the gas pedal. The truck surged forward, ramming the much smaller vehicle in the rear bumper. Skaz grinned in satisfaction as he saw the two officers jerk forward from the impact.

In the police car, Bullock fumbled for his hat as the impact knocked it onto the dashboard. Officer O'Neil made a strangled sound in the driver's seat. As Bullock reseated the hat on his head, he saw that the other man was fighting for control of the car. O'Neil lost the fight.

The police car swerved sidways, its tires smoking, seemed to balance in midair for a second, then tipped over onto its side directly in the path of the oncoming truck. Momentum carried it just beyond the tip of the truck's left bumper, and it slid back between the truck and the guard rail, sparks flying as its roof scraped along the metal rail.

Bruce watched helplessly from his position on the door. He hunched his shoulders, preparing for a deadly collision as the car neared him. The door swung almost shut seconds before the police car struck it, and Bruce gave a sigh of relief as he watched the other vehicle slide past and come to a gradual halt behind them, looking for all the world like a great, dark beetle trapped on its back.

Inside the ruined car, Bullock struggled to crawl out from under his partner, who lay sprawled unconscious on top of him. He stretched his arms out to the dash and grabbed the radio.

The right-hand door on the rear of the truck had gotten stuck about halfway open. Bruce managed to wedge himself in between the two doors, using them like a mountain climber to haul himself laboriously toward the top of the van.

When Skaz glanced back in the mirror, he saw the police car lying on its side, smoke rising from its tires. His unwanted hitchhiker was nowhere to be seen. Two birds knocked off with the same stone! He cracked an evil grin and eased up a bit on the gas pedal.

Bruce edged his way up onto the roof of the speeding vehicle, crouched for a few seconds to catch his breath, then crept forward. He began to lower himself gently onto the top of the driver's cab.

A hint of movement attracted Skaz's attention. He craned his neck, catching sight of Bruce in the small magnifier section of the rearview mirror. He slammed on his brakes.

Tires squealed as Bruce was thrust suddenly forward, dropping over the top of the cab and rolling down past the windshield to tumble over the hood. He managed to break his fall at the last moment by grab-

MASK OF THE PHANTASM

bing onto the cab's front grillwork. Skaz lifted his foot from the brake and plunged it down on the gas pedal. The truck shot forward with a complaint of steel and rubber. Bruce held on tightly. He turned his head and scanned the highway in front of them. A narrow tunnel loomed up ahead. He propped himself up on the right bumper and half climbed, half flipped himself back up onto the hood.

Bruce set his jaw and yanked the big hammer from his belt as they raced into the tunnel. Grabbing the windshield wipers with his other hand, he pulled back his arm and smashed the windshield with the hammer. The glass fractured into a spider's web of cracks. Bruce raised his arm again as the truck began to swerve wildly, caroming from side to side off the tunnel wall. Blinded by the shattered windshield, Skaz took his foot from the gas and hit the brakes once again. The truck's tires locked, smoke beginning to billow out from the wheel wells as the great vehicle skidded slowly from side to side, then came to an abrupt stop in the middle of the tunnel.

The windshield wiper cracked off in Bruce's left hand and his momentum sent him flying forward off the hood. He grabbed a piece of railing on the front grillwork and pulled his legs up from the ground just as the truck started forward again. The truck gained speed rapidly and thundered out of the tunnel, Bruce clinging to the front of the cab, his feet on the polished bumper. In the cab, Skaz cleared broken glass from the windshield frame with the edge of his sleeve. Then he reached into his jacket and hauled out his pistol. He held onto the wheel with his right hand, stuck his left through the windshield, and started firing. Bruce ducked back down against the grille as bullets struck the front edge of the hood inches above his head.

Skaz swung the steering wheel to the right, his eyes on something up ahead. The right wheels of the cab bumped up onto the curb and stayed there, riding half the sidewalk with its tires squealing. Bruce twisted his head around and froze. Twenty yards in front of them, a dozen garbage cans sat in a double row awaiting pickup. Bruce hunched his shoulders, bracing himself as best he could.

The truck plowed through the garbage cans, sending them flying in all directions as Skaz hooted in delight. Bruce took the battering along his legs and lower back. A second later the front of the cab struck a speed limit sign, flattening it instantly as Bruce cringed out of the way.

He opened the flap on one of his belt pouches and fished inside with his gloved hand. The hand came forth with half a dozen round, spiked objects. He leaned out to the left and scattered them back beneath the truck. The tiny land mines began to detonate immediately under the wheels. Four tires blew, then five, then six.

In the cab, Skaz fought for control of the steering wheel, bobbing his head to see past the web of fractured glass. The wounded truck veered wildly. Too late he saw the incline of the off ramp to the right. The truck's right front wheels dropped sharply and the huge vehicle tottered as the remaining contents of the van shifted ponderously to the right. The truck pitched over onto its side like a tranquilized elephant and began to slide down the off ramp. It pivoted on its side and headed nose first toward a concrete wall, Bruce still clinging unprotected to its grillwork. He braced himself as the wall grew before him. The screech of metal against pavement was almost deafening.

Then there was silence. Bruce opened his eyes and stared at the concrete wall inches from his face. The truck had come to a stop with less than a foot to spare. He pulled himself up onto the side of the cab and moved forward to peer in the broken window of the driver's side.

Skaz lay in a crumpled heap against the other window, moaning faintly. Glass fragments covered his contorted body.

Bruce raised his head at another sound. Three police cars came racing out of the tunnel behind them, sirens blaring and party lights flashing madly. He vaulted from the cab and ran to a nearby building, boosted himself up onto a ledge, and melted away into the shadows.

TWELVE

Mysterious Vigilante Repels Bandits

read the heading on the two-column article on page 4 of the local news section. Alfred lowered the morning paper with a small shake of his head and set it on the enameled surface of a nearby lawn table.

"I've just finished reading about your anonymous exploits last night," the butler said. "I must say, are you quite sure you won't reconsider rugby? It offers an excellent opportunity to earn the same sorts of bodily insults, and there are almost never firearms or large vehicles involved."

"Sorry, Alfred." Bruce stood several feet away on the meticulously landscaped lawn behind the mansion. He was barefoot, dressed in a white martial arts outfit. He frowned as he flowed through a series of jujitsu poses, throwing punches at an imaginary opponent. He had a large bandage across his forehead and several scratches on his face and hands. "But the plan is

MASK OF THE PHANTASM

working." He pivoted his body and launched a pair of vicious kicks into the air. "I had the edge last night. I could feel it. There was only one thing wrong."

He dropped back to a defensive stance, then fired off half a dozen punches in rapid succession. "They weren't afraid of me." He stood still, his fists clenched. "I've got to strike fear in them from the start."

"I see. Perhaps you could tell them you're from the IRS," Alfred commented drily. He glanced at the side of the mansion, his eyebrows lifting. "Pardon me, Master Bruce, but we may want to postpone any further shop talk, as it were, until later. I do believe you have a visitor."

Bruce twisted his neck to look past a screen of high bushes while maintaining his current pose, balancing on one foot with both arms extended rigidly in front of him.

"Hi there." Andrea Beaumont gave a small wave as she sauntered into view. Her eyes widened as she took in Bruce's battered and bandaged countenance. "Hey, what happened to you?" She reached in to very gently touch the edge of the bandage. "Trip over some loose cash?"

Bruce jerked back sharply at her touch. "Something like that." He turned away from her and began to work through a series of new positions. "What are you doing here?"

Alfred rolled his eyes slightly at his employer's abruptness. Andrea caught the butler's gaze with a wry smile as he left the lawn and entered the rear door of the mansion. "Well, it's been three days since we

BATMAN: THE ANIMATED MOVIE

met and still no calls," she told Bruce. "I figured you must be dead or something."

"I see." Bruce lowered his arms into his next pose. "You expect every guy you meet to call you up?"

Andrea shrugged. "Only the ones that are smart enough to dial a phone," she said matter-of-factly.

Bruce's perfect form wavered for an instant. He recovered his balance, assumed a new position, and threw a punch into the air with a low-voiced exclamation.

"Exactly what is it that you're doing?" Andrea asked.

"Jujitsu." Bruce grunted, jabbing three more times as he shifted his weight from his left foot to his right and back again.

"Gesundheit," Andrea said.

Bruce scowled in annoyance and turned slightly so that he was facing away from her.

"That was a joke," she explained.

"Jujitsu is no joke," Bruce said sternly. "It takes years of training and discipline to master." He thrust his fist out with a grunt.

Andrea had removed her sun hat. She brushed her chestnut hair back casually with her hand as she moved up behind Bruce. Then she ducked in quickly, set one hand on his shoulder, and grabbed his wrist.

"Hey!" Bruce cried as she twisted his wrist behind his back and pushed him forward. She shifted her weight and flipped him effortlessly onto the ground. "Got a few moves of my own," she observed, dusting off her palms.

"Wha—" Bruce propped himself up on his elbows,

MASK OF THE PHANTASM

blinking up at her. Andrea stood with her hands on her hips. "Miss Hovey's Self-Defense Class for Girls," she told him solemnly.

Bruce stared up at her without expression. Then the corner of his mouth curled up, and the next moment he had started chuckling. Andrea's mouth dropped open in mock astonishment.

"He laughs!" she exclaimed. "And from a supine position. Now, *that* takes training and discipline."

Bruce stopped laughing. He arched an eyebrow at Andrea, then swept his feet suddenly in a wide arc, tripping her. She tumbled backward onto the soft grass. Before she could move, Bruce had her pinned down, nose to nose. She looked up at him in surprise as they broke into matching grins.

"Nice footwork," Andrea said. "Can you dance, too?"

Bruce's grin grew thoughtful as he lowered his face toward hers.

At that moment, the rear door of the mansion swung open and Alfred emerged carrying a tray of orangeade and cookies. Spying the couple on the lawn, the butler made a smooth U-turn and stepped back inside the house while the door was still in mid-swing.

Bruce and Andrea smiled into each other's eyes, oblivious of Alfred's brief appearance, and wondered what would happen next. . . .

Bruce stood at the fireplace in his study, his eyes focused on the leaping flames, his thoughts lost in memory. There was a tap at the door behind him and

Alfred stepped in. Off-key piano music entered the room after him.

"Pardon me, sir," the butler said primly. "But Miss Barbara and Miss Penny have begun dancing on top of the piano."

"Brucie!" a woman called plaintively from the other room. "Where have you gotten to?"

Bruce sighed and crossed the room toward the door.

THIRTEEN

The limousine prowled slowly down the puddled roadway, its headlights shining before it in streaks of yellow-gold. An owl hooted twice from the towering oak at the edge of the cemetery, took wing, and flapped off into the night. Leaves were blowing across the damp pavement as the limo pulled up to the gates and stopped.

The front doors opened and two men climbed out. They were both stocky, with thick shoulders and grim expressions. The man on the driver's side stretched and nudged his door shut as the other man carefully scanned the area. The passenger moved to the rear door and pulled it open.

A half-smoked cigar dropped out onto the pavement with a faint sizzle. Then a tall, imposing man in his early sixties exited the car and stood, pulling on a pair of expensive-looking leather gloves.

"Buzz" Bronski—known as Joseph only on his birth certificate and driver's license—glanced at one of the burly bodyguards and held his left hand out expectantly. The big man reached into the backseat and handed his boss a black funeral wreath studded with small velvet bows. Buzz transferred the wreath to the crook of his right arm and held out his left hand again. This time the bodyguard handed him a large silver flashlight. Buzz clicked the flashlight on and waved it experimentally at the nearest trees. "You guys wait here," he said to the two men.

The man on the passenger side nodded vigorously. "Whatever you say, Mr. Bronski." He and his partner leaned back against the car and watched as their boss headed off through the big black iron gates.

The owl hooted again from somewhere inside the cemetery. The driver's eyes darted left and right. "Jeez, ya don't have ta pay me ta stay in the car in this kinda neighborhood," he said, pulling out a cigarette and tapping it on the steering wheel.

"Me neither," said his partner. "Cemeteries are for stiffs, that's what I say." Thunder rolled in the distance.

"They're sayin' the Bat iced this guy." The driver stuck the cigarette in his mouth and struck a match.

"I know. Who'd a' thought." Just then a rustling sound came from the bushes just inside the iron fence. "What was that?" The two men craned their necks at the line of dark foliage.

"I dunno, but it—*oww!*" The driver shook his hand as the match burned the ends of his fingers. Both match and cigarette dropped to the ground. "Jeez," the bodyguard said again, sticking his fingertips in his mouth.

MASK OF THE PHANTASM

Inside the cemetery, Buzz Bronski followed his flashlight beam along a narrow path. There was no sound except the crunching of his shoes on the coarse gravel. Finally the pale beam picked out a newly installed headstone with a single dimestore vase of red and white carnations at its base. Bronski played the light over the granite monument. " 'Charlton'?" he said to himself. "You're kidding. . . ." He heaved a sigh, then tossed the funeral wreath toward his former associate's final resting place. The black ring sailed through the air like a life preserver and struck the base of the small vase, tipping it over onto its side. Water and carnations spilled onto the grass.

"*Tsk, tsk.* Chuckie, Chuckie." Bronski shook his head over the new grave. "You always were a loser." He was turning back toward the path when a faint sound caught his attention.

"*Buzz . . . Buzz Bronski . . .*" the voice was eerie, filtered in some manner that made it sound like the droning speech of a living computer.

Bronski stiffened and reached into his coat pocket. "Who's there?" He waved the flashlight in a wide arc in the direction of the sound. There was a black mist rising out of the ground around a cluster of nearby graves. Bronski shone the flashlight into the billowing cloud. A pale flash of movement showed suddenly at the center of the circle of yellow light.

"*Your angel of death awaits,*" the unearthly voice intoned, as a grinning death's head mask emerged from behind a weathered gravestone, as if rising directly from the netherworld. The head drifted forward as if it were floating on the black mist.

"Huh?" Bronski took several steps backward. His heel hit something solid and he turned to shine the light down on the vase lying near Chuckie Sol's headstone. When he lifted it again in the direction of the ring of graves, both mist and skull had vanished. Bronski pushed his hat back on his head and scratched his scalp.

"Buzz Bronski . . ." This time the voice came from much closer. Bronski wheeled around, the flashlight wavering in his grip. The death's head hung to his right above a cloud of black mist. Bronski scowled and pointed the light directly beneath the floating skull. The beam slanted away into the mist as if it had been deflected in some fashion. The skull floated toward him, and he could make out a long, ragged cloak hanging below it. The cloak parted when it was several feet away. Something sharp and metallic gleamed in the flashlight beam.

"Who the—" Bronski started to back away again, his broad features contorting in fear. "Get away from me, ya freak!" He turned and raced past Sol's headstone, his heavy shoe scattering the carnations and crushing red and white petals into the newly turned earth.

Bronski's labored breathing broke the stillness of the cemetery as he raced over the sloping lawns, his flashlight beam darting frantically in front of him. Which way was the gate? Was that a footstep behind him? His heart pounded in his chest as he mounted an unfamiliar rise. He stopped for a moment and bent over, hands on his knees, breath coming in gasps. A twig snapped on his left and he lumbered forward

MASK OF THE PHANTASM

again. As he started down the other side of the hillock, his knee collided with something hard. The flashlight flew into the air and Bronski fought for balance, his arms flailing. He pitched over onto his side, coming down hard against an abandoned wheelbarrow piled with sod and digging implements. He ended up on his back, the wheelbarrow upside down on the lower half of his body. As he tipped it back onto its wheels and pushed himself up from the damp grass, his hand brushed against a sturdy wooden handle. He felt along its length, encountering a perpendicular sweep of cold metal. A pick! Bronski crawled to his feet and hefted the implement above his head with a small grunt of satisfaction. He took a step forward, brandishing the pick like a weapon. "Where are ya *now*, ya freak?" he blustered to the empty darkness.

"*Now indeed, Mr. Bronski . . .*" The voice came from directly behind him. "*Now is the time to pay for your considerable sins. . . .*"

Bronski whirled around. There it was! He charged forward, slicing through the dark mist with the pick. The skull mask drifted back into the roiling clouds and vanished.

"*Over here . . .*" This time the death's head hung in a cloud of mist to his left. He swung again, panting with exertion, and again the floating mask melted back into the concealing vapor. Bronski wiped the perspiration from his brow. "How—?"

"*This way, Mr. Bronski. . . .*" The thing stood in the shadow of a grove of tall black trees with skeletal branches. As Bronski watched, it raised its right arm and motioned to him with the wicked metal claw he

BATMAN: THE ANIMATED MOVIE

had glimpsed earlier. Bronski swallowed, looking from the sharp curve of metal to the pick he held in his hands. Then he straightened his shoulders and charged toward the apparition. "All right, you creep! Let's see what ya do with this!"

Mist rose and the dark figure seemed to drift backward, leading him on. Then suddenly it was right alongside him. There was a flash of metal in the darkness and a cracking sound. Bronski staggered back as a sudden jolt traveled up his arms. His eyes bulged as he watched the head of the pick sail through the dimness and embed itself in the ground in front of a small headstone. He looked at the shaft he still held gripped in his hands: the wood had been sliced neatly in two just below the blade.

"*Buzz . . .*" He stiffened when he heard his name again. He lowered the stick, clutching it protectively in front of his chest. The apparition was in front of him, floating toward him on a boiling cloud of black mist. Bronski wavered, then stood his ground. He drew his arm back as the thing neared him, then flung the shaft of wood at it with an inarticulate cry of rage.

The dark figure raised its ragged arms and the stick disappeared silently into the roiling mist. Then the death's head appeared again. "*You always were a loser, Mr. Bronski. . . .*" Once again the creature advanced on him.

Bronski turned and stumbled off into the darkness. He ran without looking back, until his heart and lungs could stand it no more. He collapsed on his knees at the side of an ancient headstone, trying to catch his breath until a small sound at his back made him look over his shoulder, eyes wide with panic. It was still coming.

He pushed to his feet, leaning heavily on the gravestone, then took a deep breath and pounded up a low hill to his right. He must be nearing the fence. He saw a dim figure standing near the top of the hill. It was dressed in pale garments, its head turned away from him, and there was no mist billowing around its legs. A caretaker? Bronski wondered. A gravedigger? Could he be close to the gate? Maybe it was one of the boys, come looking for him. He trudged up the hill, squinting intently at the dim outline. When he was a few feet away he saw that it was a huge stone angel, its arms raised in an attitude of prayer. He took another step forward—

And was falling.

He landed with a heavy thud a second later. Bronski lay facedown on a patch of wet, muddy ground, his thoughts whirling, the wind knocked out of his heavy body. He raised his head, mud dripping from his cheeks and brow, and pushed himself to his knees. He looked up.

Buzz Bronski was kneeling six feet down, at the bottom of a freshly dug grave. Directly above him, the stone angel loomed pitilessly over the open pit. He heard a soft snapping sound and turned to look at the other end of the grave. A dark mist began to flow over the edge of the opening as he watched, obscuring the night sky. As it dispersed, a tall black figure with a pale skull for a head became gradually visible. The death's head floated above him, collared in mist.

Bronski gasped and heaved awkwardly to his feet.

BATMAN: THE ANIMATED MOVIE

He stumbled toward the angel at the other end of the grave and began to claw at the soft loam above his head. His fingers pulled clods of earth down onto his mud-streaked face. His right hand struck the base of the stone angel and he began to sob.

"Farewell, Mr. Bronski. . ." The eerie voice faded in volume as if the apparition were receding into the distance. Bronski turned around to find the far end of the pit empty except for a haze of dispersing mist. He blinked up at the stars for a few seconds, dumbfounded. He thought he heard another sound, faint, nearby. He looked back and forth between the ends of the trench. Nothing. Maybe the thing had just wanted to frighten him, after all. He leaned his palm against the side of the pit for support as he fished for a handkerchief in his coat and wiped the cold sweat from his forehead. The faint sound came again. He searched the edges of the trench where the masked apparition had stood, eyes narrowed. Behind him, a tiny curl of black mist appeared at the base of the towering stone monument. A pebble slipped forward and dropped into the grave with a muffled sound as the base tilted slightly. Bronski looked over his shoulder as the shadow of the angel crawled slowly up his back.

"No!" His eyes filled with terror and he raised his arm in a futile gesture. The handkerchief fluttered to the ground. *"No!"*

The driver plucked his fourth cigarette unlit from his dry lips and glanced wide-eyed at his partner. The faraway scream seemed to come from deep inside the cemetery. A muffled crash sounded, then all was silent. "Jeez," said the driver.

"C'mon!" The other man pushed open the passenger door and scrambled out of the car. The driver tossed his cigarette out the window and followed more slowly.

It took them several minutes to draw a bead on the source of the scream. They were stumbling through the darkness, calling for their boss, when the driver's shin struck the edge of the wheelbarrow. When he stopped with a curse to massage it, he saw a pale yellow glow shining on the ground from beneath a clump of ornamental shrubbery. "Hey—it's his flashlight!"

Using the light, they were able to follow the dark prints Buzz Bronski's rapid footsteps had left in the dewy grass. Moments later they were mounting a low hill near the heart of the cemetery. The driver looked around anxiously. The stars seemed cold and tiny, and the rim of the dark sky was shrouded with pale clouds.

"Here they are—over this way!" His partner waved to him. The footprints led them to a long trench that seemed to be partially filled with something. The other man stood peering downward. "Bring that light over here, will ya?"

The driver joined him at the edge of the pit and aimed the beam downward. "Oh." The driver stepped back from the grave, the flashlight slipping from his nerveless fingers. "Oh, man."

The second bodyguard turned away from the pit with his hand over his mouth. Out of the corner of his eye, he saw a flash of movement. A dark shape stood atop a far-off hillock, its bowed head silhouetted

BATMAN: THE ANIMATED MOVIE

against the just-rising moon. A long black cape fluttered in the breeze.

"It's the Bat!" yelled the driver. "It's the stinkin' Bat! Jeez!" He lifted his revolver and started firing furiously at the dark figure. After a second's hesitation, his partner drew his own weapon and dropped to one knee, aiming carefully along his arm as he, too, opened fire.

With a swirl of ragged cape, the dark intruder vanished into the night.

FOURTEEN

The town house was located not far from Park Row, the once-fashionable section of downtown Gotham now known as Crime Alley. Because of its proximity to an area where burglary and murder were daily occurrences, the windows of the old brownstone were covered with black bars of wrought iron, lending a prisonlike air to the somber building which persisted even in the bright light of morning.

Sunlight fell in measured blocks onto the worn arabesques and faded geometries of an ancient Persian rug inside the shadowy den that centered the top floor apartment. The room was silent except for the irregular clinking sound caused by metal against porcelain and the equally irregular susurrus of an old man's breathing.

Salvatore Valestra sat hunched over in a chair that had grown much too large for him. A plastic tray stood before him on spidery metal legs, and on the

BATMAN: THE ANIMATED MOVIE

tray were a cup of pale yellow tea, a bowl containing one half of a small pink grapefruit, and a copy of the morning *Times*. The old man took the spoon from the cup and set it carefully on the saucer. Then he brought the cup to his pursed lips and sipped at its rim. His face was an unhealthy color, the sallow skin pulled parchment-tight across the planes of bone beneath.

Valestra reseated the cup with trembling fingers and turned his attention to the pinkish hemisphere that constituted this morning's breakfast. He maneuvered a slice of the tart fruit onto his spoon and mumbled it past his lips as he unfolded the newspaper. He blinked in surprise as he scanned the front page. In the center of the page was a file photograph of a round-faced man with cold eyes and an angry sneer: Joseph "Buzz" Bronski. Valestra's eyes grew wide in their sunken sockets as he read the bold headline:

SECOND GANGSTER SLAIN

A sketchy artist's rendering of a dramatic dark figure shrouded in a long cloak appeared next to the second caption:

HAS BAT GONE BATS?

The spoonful of grapefruit slipped unnoticed from the old man's skeletal fingers and clattered onto the plastic tray top. "No!" Valestra began to wheeze, clutching at his throat. "No!" he cried again, bolting out of the chair, the paper falling to one side as the tray collapsed on the other. He stood for a few confused seconds, his glance darting from window to doorway to window. But where was there to run to? His wheezing grew more frantic, and he staggered back to the overstuffed chair and leaned on it for support. He felt at the back of the chair for the cool surface of the oxygen tank, dragged it out, and fumbled the plastic mask free from its coil of clear tubing. He stretched the mask up to cover his nose and mouth. Exhausted by his exertions, he slumped back into the chair, breathing in spasmodic gasps. His rheumy eyes stared down in terror at the newspaper scattered on the carpet.

FIFTEEN

"**W**hat do you mean, you won't? You *have* to go after him!"

The sunset was a brilliant abstract in scarlet and crimson outside the window of Commissioner James Gordon's office. Its beauty went unnoticed by Councilman Arthur Reeves, whose face was also several shades of red. Reeves was in the midst of shaking an accusatory finger at Gordon, all the while haranguing the older man in his best fire-and-brimstone style.

The commissioner sat impassively behind his desk.

"He didn't do it." Gordon stated his response matter-of-factly, making Reeves's histrionics seem all the more out of place. Behind the councilman's back, several high-level police officers exchanged glances as they watched the encounter between their boss and his outraged adversary.

"Look, *Mr.* Gordon, you've got two eyewitnesses—" Reeves wheeled around and snatched a double ribbon of polygraph recording paper from the large hands of Detective Harvey Bullock. Each length of paper was attached to an unflattering mug shot of one of Buzz Bronski's henchmen. "—*And* their lie detector results." He flung the records down on Gordon's cluttered blotter. "What more do you need?"

Gordon rose behind his desk, his own anger finally beginning to show in his face. He swept the tangle of papers and photographs from his desk and into the wastebasket with a savage motion of his mind. "It's garbarge, *Mr.* Reeves," he snarled. "Batman does *not* kill. Period." He strode to his office door, turned back to face the fuming councilman. "You want him—*you* get him. There's no motive, no proof, and I'll have no part of spending the taxpayers' money to bring him in." He jerked the door open and exited into the hall.

The door slammed shut behind him with a resounding noise. The assembled officers flinched, Detective Bullock eyeing the door's pebbled glass window as if waiting for it to shatter. When it remained intact, he pulled a small wooden toothpick from his rumpled jacket and stuck it in the corner of his mouth with a sigh.

Reeves turned back to those who remained in the room. He plucked a small vial of breath freshener from the inside pocket of his jacket and sprayed it twice into the back of his mouth. Then he set his jaw. "Well, gentlemen," he said softly. "Any ideas?"

Unseen in the shadows just outside Gordon's window, a gray-and-black figure crouched motionless on the narrow ledge of stone. After several minutes, Batman removed a small listening device from the side of his mask and straightened, a frown of frustration on

BATMAN: THE ANIMATED MOVIE

his face. He fired a grapple into the night and swung off above the city, a black bird of prey silhouetted against the wild sunset.

Minutes later, Councilman Reeves accompanied a contingent of high-ranking officers out onto the roof of police headquarters. A dark blue tarpaulin was removed from an odd-looking device mounted on the rooftop, and adjustments were made at its base. Then a switch was thrown, and a bright yellow beam lanced upward into the darkening sky. A golden oval surrounding the dramatic emblem of a black bat flashed onto a bank of high clouds.

Councilman Reeves leaned back against the uneven brickwork of a nearby chimney and waited for the Dark Knight's arrival. The officers stood in a loose circle around him, their expressions betraying their misgivings as they scanned the empty skies. The minutes ticked by.

"Jeez . . ." Bullock wiped a smudge from the crystal of his wristwatch and angled it to catch the last rays of sunlight. "He's usually pretty punctual."

The sleek black vehicle called the Batmobile barreled away from the twilight city, its grim-faced driver eyeing the Bat Signal in the outside mirror.

Half an hour later, the fantastic car was parked carefully out of sight not far from the cemetery where mobster Buzz Bronski had met his angel of death for the first and last time.

Strips of yellow police tape cordoned off the scene of Bronski's demise. The massive statue hung suspended above the trench in a thick bundle of chains attached to a cranelike vehicle.

The Dark Knight had begun his investigation by retracing Bronski's trail from his limo to the gravesite. He surveyed the scene of the overturned wheelbarrow on bended knee.

"There appears to be some chemical residue on the lawn. Could match the traces I found on the fragments of windshield glass at the parking garage." He spoke softly into a button microphone connected by a slender wire to his utility belt. "Not much to go on," he concluded, "but it's been that kind of day." He clicked off the microphone and allowed the wire to draw it back into its compartment on his gold belt. Something caught his eye and he turned his head in surprise, looking at his surroundings as if seeing them from a new angle.

Not far from the tatters of police tape stood a tall granite obelisk. Batman rose and moved toward it. He touched the marble of the Wayne monument with his gloved hand, his eyes lowered.

"They call it 'perpetual care.' You'd think they could at least afford a weed eater. . . ."

The Dark Knight's head came up in shock. He took a step back and peered through the dimness between two other monuments.

A young woman in a dark suit knelt at a neglected grave, her fists tugging at a clump of stubborn weeds that had sprouted at the base of the headstone. "Sorry, Mom," the woman murmured. "Seems like the whole world's going to seed." She started at the sound of a twig snapping and turned to look over her shoulder.

BATMAN: THE ANIMATED MOVIE

She saw a man dressed in black and gray, standing in the shadows next to a tall monument. A look of barely controlled anguish was visible on the portion of his face not covered by the black mask. He wavered for a moment, watching her, then stepped back into the deepening dusk.

The woman rose to her feet, the weeds dropping from her fingers. "No," she said under her breath, watching the dark figure's retreat. She moved across the sloping lawn and halted by the monument, her fingers tracing the name carved into its face as she stared off into the twilight.

"Bruce . . ." Andrea Beaumont whispered to the deserted cemetery.

SIXTEEN

According to its tastefully illustrated brochure, the recently opened Gotham Sheridan Hotel provided an ideal marriage of luxury and convenience to both the busy executive and the seasoned world traveler. Its 722 guest rooms included thirty suites, all of which featured TV/VCRs, complimentary minibars, and exquisite service. A new four-star restaurant capped the Sheridan's soaring tower. Chez Felice's picture windows offered a panoramic view of the city, while its menu was an expensive compendium of the smart set's trendiest delicacies.

The maître d' looked as if he had been transferred to the real world directly from the pages of *Haute Cuisine* magazine. He inclined his perfectly groomed head to his newest guests and conducted them to their elegantly set table as if he were bringing holy pilgrims to a shrine.

Councilman Arthur Reeves followed close behind Andrea as they crossed the room, talking rapidly in a

BATMAN: THE ANIMATED MOVIE

low voice. The object of his monologue walked among the tables with her eyes on the polished floor, lost in thought."

". . . so I'm having the banker cut through a hundred yards or so of red tape," Reeves said. "He tells me he'll have no problem rolling your money into a higher yield account."

"Amount . . . ?" Andrea nodded politely as the maître d' held her chair for her. "Thank you." She sat and turned to Reeves with a bewildered expression. "What amount?"

"Account." Reeves smiled indulgently. "I was telling you about my herculean efforts on behalf of your financial well-being."

"I'm sorry, Arthur." Andrea forced a sheepish grin. "Being back in Gotham's still a little overwhelming." Her hand wandered up to rest over the gold locket for a moment. "I guess I was . . . reminiscing."

"Hey, that's okay. I know you must have a lot on your mind." Reeves leaned back in his chair as a waiter appeared with menus. He flashed Andrea a magnanimous smile. "What's important is that you take your time and get your priorities in order. For example: what wine shall we start with tonight?"

Gargoyles crouched menacingly along the cathedral's high ledge, their ire seemingly directed at the broad windows of Chez Felice across the avenue. Lightning streaked the sky, revealing a smaller figure hunkered down among the devil shapes. Thunder rolled beneath the clouds as the Dark Knight shifted positions, perching atop a buttress where he would be partially concealed by a jutting stone wing, while still having a clear view of the restaurant. The wind blew his cape into a black fan along the gargoyle's pitted flank.

Settled on his windswept perch, Batman drew a pair of miniature high-powered binoculars from his utility belt and trained them on the building across the street. In the window of the softly lit restaurant, a man and woman in evening dress were toasting each other with glasses filled with pale gold. The man on the ledge adjusted his binoculars and leaned forward, watching.

Reeves ordered for himself and then for Andrea— who considered the custom archaic and patronizing, but had decided to allow him the transgression this once, since he had made it clear he was paying for the meal. The waiter approved their choices and exited with a small bow.

"Remember this place?" Reeves asked, his eyes on her face with its dramatic cheekbones and startling blue-green eyes.

"Of course I do." Andrea smiled politely. "You and Daddy and I used to come here all the time."

Reeves allowed a touch of concern to creep into his voice: "How *is* the old fellow?" he asked.

Andrea glanced at the window, where lightning was beginning to stab beyond the saw-toothed skyline of dark buildings. A trick of the light made it seem as if one of the gargoyles twitched its dark wing against the mounting wind. "He hasn't got a care in the world," she said quietly.

"Ah." Reeves nodded benevolently. "You and he are still close, I take it?"

"Closer than ever." Her smile seemed to falter for a moment, then returned.

"I'm sorry your dad couldn't make it into town this time," Reeves said into the silence that followed. After a slight hesitation, he reached across the snowy tablecloth and placed his hands on hers. "But then, I've always wished I could have some time alone with you."

"Well . . ." Andrea met his gaze, her mouth turned up at the corner. She gazed down at his hands, allowing them to remain where they were. "Who knows what the future might bring?" she said at last.

SEVENTEEN

Across the avenue from Chez Felice, the Dark Knight lowered the tiny binoculars. Rain dripped from the black cowl and ran in rivulets along the folds of his cape. A flash of lightning captured an expression on his face that could almost have been pain. Thunder rumbled as the heart of the storm approached quickly from the south. He leaned back against the cathedral wall, memories flooding his thoughts. . . .

The distant rumbling noise grew louder as the futuristic monorail shot past the young couple on its tour of the fairgrounds. Marveling, they watched its sleek silver length disappear beneath a banner proclaiming

GOTHAM WORLD'S FAIR

A polished voice resonated through the public address system as they strolled hand in hand along an

BATMAN: THE ANIMATED MOVIE

arched walkway toward the fair's Main Plaza: "Welcome, ladies and gentlemen, boys and girls, to a dream of the future, a bright tomorrow filled with hope and promise for all. This is a vision of the shimmering utopia where we shall all spend the rest of our lives. . . ."

The couple exchanged happy smiles, pausing at the Main Plaza to admire the fair's centerpiece, a beautifully wrought globe of a ringed planet mounted next to a stylized spaceship poised for flight on its scalloped fins. The Omniglobe and the Astroplane were the fair's symbols, available on everything from playing cards to commemorative dessert spoons.

Bordering the Main Plaza was a ring of diverse eating establishments collectively known as the Gastronomical Observatory. Here visitors could witness the creation of new and exciting culinary marvels—and then sample those that appealed to them.

The young couple sat at a small table before the star-dappled facade of the Heavenly Ice Cream Café. They sat side by side, holding each other's hands while trying to maneuver their ice cream cones.

Andrea nudged Bruce's elbow as they started on their cones. A plump young man about five years their senior was seated at the next table with an older man and woman—also plump, and probably his parents. He was eating a concoction of bananas and pastel-colored frozen yogurt piled high in a long plastic boat.

"Y'know, I got to where I could make one of these without even checking the directions," the young man remarked. " 'Course we called 'em Banana Buddies instead of Star Boats, and Mr. Datwillig always skimped a bit on the cherries.''

His parents exchanged glances. ''Burton, have you given any more thought to what that nice man at the job booth said?'' his mother inquired hesitantly. ''About writing travel brochures or looking into that correspondence course in cartography?''

The young man set down his Star Boat and leaned his elbows on the table top. ''I don't want to write about faraway places, and I don't want to draw them on the map so somebody else can find them,'' he said, staring up at the Astroplane with a dreaming look in his eyes. ''I want to *visit* them.''

''Here we go again,'' his father said with a sigh. The older man checked his watch. ''We'd better get going, Mother. We've got a two-hour drive ahead of us, and 'What's That Song?' comes on at nine o'clock sharp.''

Andrea gave Bruce's hand a squeeze as the trio cleared off their table and departed. Her eyes sparkled with amusement. ''Now, that's the kind of son most parents hope for,'' she said when they were out of earshot. ''Easygoing, dependable, and a master of the Star Boat.''

''Except Mr. Datwillig made them skimp on the cherries,'' Bruce said. ''Is that the kind of son you would hope for?''

''Oh, I think I'd want my child to be a little more adventurous at that age.'' Andrea pursed her lips, turning to watch the plump threesome as they squeezed out through the turnstile to the parking lot.

BATMAN: THE ANIMATED MOVIE

"Hurrying home to watch 'What's That Song?' with the folks. . . ." She shook her head.

"He said he wanted to visit faraway places," Bruce said judiciously. "I'd say that's adventurous."

"Ah, but when? Didn't you catch the note of desperation in Mom's voice? I'd say they're more than ready to help junior start his exploration of the great unknown."

Bruce was silent for a few moments. "It must be great, watching your kids grow up," he said.

Andrea nodded, her eyes on his face. She took a long lick from the side of her ice cream cone and held it out to him.

"Here. Want to try some of mine?" she asked. " 'Plutonian peanut butter with comet sprinkles'—it's actually pretty good."

Bruce shook his head. "Mine's fine, thanks." He glanced down at the menu visible on the tabletop beneath a thin plastic lamination. "Tastiest 'Mars-mallow chocolate' I've ever had."

"Chocolate is boring, Bruce. Be adventurous. Visit faraway places." With a mischievous grin, Andrea thrust her cone at Bruce's mouth, smearing his lips and cheeks with the gooey tan confection.

"Hey!" Bruce reached out as she jumped to her feet and skipped away from the table. Then she darted back in and tugged at his sleeve. "C'mon," she said. "Your face is covered with goop. We'd better get you inside one of these pavilions before everybody starts pointing at you." She drew her forefinger along his upper lip and licked at it playfully. "You know, you wouldn't look half bad with a mustache." She turned and trotted off toward a nearby building.

Bruce drew his handkerchief from his pocket and dabbed at the ice cream. He shook his head in feigned exasperation and took off after Andrea.

She stopped at the bottom of the steps of the great hall and stretched her arm out to him. Bruce slipped his hand into hers with a grin and they started up the steps together.

Yard-high letters mounted on the curving roof read

FORWARD TO THE FUTURE

Four arched doorways fronted the building. Above each doorway sat a smiling, ten-foot-tall mechanical man, jointed legs straddling the archway and left arm raised in greeting. Bruce and Andrea passed inside to find themselves beneath a vast segmented dome. The four paths from the doorways converged at the loading platform of a narrow track. A fleet of two-passenger, aerodynamic cars moved noiselessly nose to tail along the track, which followed a circuitous route that brought visitors on a tour of the entire complex. Bruce and Andrea hurried to the next car in line and scrambled inside.

The car climbed a gradually ascending ramp, then headed out across a trestled bridge above a miniature City of the Future. They gazed in amazement as football-sized autogyros hovered like overgrown hummingbirds among twelve- and fifteen-foot skyscrapers, while inch-long automobiles flowed in

complicated traffic patterns on the eight-lane boule-
vards below.

The car passed between two raised stages occupied
by animated dolls who smiled and waved at the passengers. The dolls were a careful mix of races and
cultures, wearing futuristic versions of international
costumes. The car slowed to a crawl as music came
from concealed speakers and the silver-clad automa-
tons burst into song:

> "Forward, Gotham, to the future,
> Our dreams are shining bright.
> Glory and wonder surround us,
> A new tomorrow is in sight."

Bruce found himself growing quickly bored with
the singers' treacly lyrics and unrelenting cuteness. He
turned around in the car, trying to get a closer look at
the diminutive autogyros buzzing around the model
city. Andrea caught his glance and rolled her eyes.
They covered their ears with their palms and grinned
at each other as the car accelerated slightly and entered another area of the exhibit.

The House of the Future was mostly glass and filled
with gadgets. The main living area was divided into
two sections by the narrow track. On their right an
android housewife with blank eyes and stylized
golden curls methodically chopped plastic vegetables
in her ultramodern kitchenette. Across the tracks, her
husband reclined on a silvery sofa. A small robot dog
that looked like it had been assembled from an Erector
Set yapped and wagged its tail as the car moved

MASK OF THE PHANTASM

slowly by. The android husband looked up from his newspaper long enough to wave to the riders. Behind them, the dolls began a new chorus:

> "With heart and hope to light the way,
> We'll welcome in a brand-new day!
> Forward, Gotham, to the future,
> The future starts today."

Andrea inspected the ceaselessly chopping android wife with skepticism as they trundled by. "Hope she gets time off to watch 'What's That Song?'" she grumbled. Double doors opened ahead of them and they left the House of the Future and its cloying melodies with relief. Andrea leaned against Bruce as he helped her from the car, and they stood that way for a few seconds, her head against his chest and his arms clasped around her. They disengaged with a warm smile and walked on.

The Hall of Transportation was a sprawling, high-ceilinged pavilion, open at the sides to allow the great ribbon of the fair's monorail track to pass in and out. Massive columns supported the curving roof. Inside, a spiraling ramp led them down inside a transparent rocket shape, which was suspended inside a cavernous silo by three sideward struts. The struts had walkways on their upper surfaces. Depending on which walkway they chose, visitors disembarking from the ramp headed toward one of three different exhibit clusters.

Bruce and Andrea walked toward a platform advertising the Automobile of the Future. Above them, single-person autogyros soared and dipped beneath the

BATMAN: THE ANIMATED MOVIE

ceiling. The monorail rumbled by as they neared the platform, and they leaned against the railing of the walkway to watch its rapid passage. Andrea's eyes shone with anticipation.

"Do you think we'll really see any of this in our lifetime?" she asked. Bruce opened his mouth to reply. Then something caught his attention and he moved from her side, drawn to the exhibit on the platform like a moth to a flourescent bulb.

"Bruce?" Andrea walked after him.

The Automobile of the Future was mounted on a slowly turning pedestal at the center of the exhibit. It was long and sleek, with a bubble cockpit and flaring fins. A modified jet engine protruded from its tail. When Andrea caught up with Bruce he was staring raptly at the fantastic vehicle, his eyes tracing its sinuous lines. "A jet thruster," he murmured to himself. "Incredible . . ."

"Bruce?" She stepped in behind him, slipping her arm through his. "Bruce, I was talking to you."

"Huh?" He turned to face her with a sheepish expression, jolted out of his reverie. "Oh, I'm sorry, Andi. My mind was on . . . something else . . ."

"Oh, really?" Andrea arched her eyebrows as the two skirted the turning pedestal and headed out of the exhibit. She glanced around the platform at the other visitors. "Like what?"

"Hmm?" Bruce looked at her blankly.

"You said your mind was on something else," she prompted.

"Oh, just . . . you know . . ." They left the Hall of Transportation. Up ahead, an arching sign that di-

MASK OF THE PHANTASM

rected visitors back across the midway to the model city was emblazoned with the words: "Enter Gotham of the Future." Bruce pointed to the sign. "The future."

"Ah." Andrea smiled playfully. "Anyone's in particular? Or just the generic variety?"

"*You* know. . . ." They passed hand in hand through a bank of turnstiles and exited the fairgrounds. Bruce's limousine awaited them in the parking lot, conspicuous among the more modest cars that surrounded it.

"No, I don't," Andrea said. "When was the last time you talked to *me* about any of your plans?"

Alfred Pennyworth was standing smartly at attention in his chauffeur's uniform next to the driver's side door of the limo. Andrea hung back a little. "Y'know," she said quietly, turning to rest her hands on Bruce's chest, "Dad's been wanting to meet you."

"Oh, yeah?" Bruce tried to keep his expression neutral.

"Mm-hmm." Andrea inspected his left lapel. "But I told him you're not up to it yet," she added nonchalantly, watching him carefully from the corner of her eye.

"Um. I wouldn't say that." Bruce gave a wary shrug. "I can meet him—I mean if you want me to."

"Great!" Andrea stood up on tiptoe and gave him a quick kiss. Then she released his jacket and strode toward the limo. "I'll call him right now!"

When Bruce reached the car, Andrea was already seated in the back, punching in a number on the

BATMAN: THE ANIMATED MOVIE

limo's telephone. She looked up at him as she brought the receiver to her ear. "You're sure about this?"

Bruce summoned up a smile. "Sure I'm sure," he told her. He stepped back to stand next to Alfred as Andrea began to speak excitedly into the phone. "Alfred," he whispered, "what the heck am I doing? *This* isn't part of the plan!" He rubbed his forehead in confusion. "I must be going crazy."

Alfred relaxed his stiff posture long enough to tilt his head toward his employer. "If I may be so bold, Master Bruce, I'd say quite the reverse. . . ."

"We're set," Andrea announced brightly, leaning her head out of the car. "Dad says later this afternoon would be fine."

"Great," Bruce said, hoping his manufactured enthusiasm would pass for genuine.

"Mm-hm." Andrea looked him up and down speculatively. "This gives Alfred and me time to find you something to wear."

"What?" Bruce looked down at his casual slacks and jacket. "You mean I can't go like this?"

"Oh, Alfred . . ." Andrea rolled her eyes at the butler, who had allowed a slight smile to creep onto his narrow face. "How do you put up with this guy?"

EIGHTEEN

Carl Beaumont's office
was located on the sixteenth floor of the Peterson
Building, an imposing structure that fronted a wide
avenue in Gotham's riverside financial district. Half a
block down from the building, an auto-and-pedestrian
bridge spanned the Gotham River itself.

Beaumont was a businessman in his early fifties, a
tall, handsome man with an aristocratic air. At three
o'clock in the afternoon, he was sitting behind a dark
mahogany desk riffling through a stack of legal documents.

"Sir, if you could go over these as well. . . ."
Twenty-three-year-old Arthur Reeves stood to one
side of the mammoth desk and offered Beaumont
another file.

A figure appeared in the open doorway as Beaumont spread the documents on his blotter. "Knock-
knock," said Andrea.

Beaumont looked up from the desk, his face

BATMAN: THE ANIMATED MOVIE

brightening instantly at the sight of his daughter. He straightened his tie with one hand and pushed his pile of work to the side with the other. Reeves intercepted the file folder as it slid precariously close to the edge of the desk. He cradled it in his arms and stepped back with a small frown of irritation.

"Well," Beaumont walked around the desk. "This is a most pleasant interruption."

Andrea beamed at her father as she and Bruce entered the room arm in arm. She gave Bruce a gentle nudge forward as Beaumont crossed the room to greet them.

"Ah, at last I meet the elusive Bruce Wayne." Beaumont stuck out his hand and Bruce shook it awkwardly.

"Nice to meet you, sir."

" 'Sir'?" The older man cocked his eyebrow reprovingly at Bruce. "Don't be so formal, son. Andrea's told me so much about you, I feel like we're practically family."

Andrea cleared her throat and shot a disapproving glance at her father. "Daddy . . ."

A rustling sound broke the awkward silence that followed, as Arthur Reeves gathered up a sheaf of papers from Beaumont's desk and tucked them under his arm. The others turned to him.

"Oh, don't mind me," Reeves said stiffly. "I was just leaving." Beaumont nodded at the young man as he passed them on his way to the door. "Oh, I'm sorry. This is Arthur Reeves, one of the hot young turks from my legal department." Reeves halted and shook hands obediently with Bruce. "He's someone

MASK OF THE PHANTASM

you should get to know," Beaumont added. "Young Arthur here is going places."

On bustling Scott Avenue some sixteen stories below, a long black sedan pulled over to the curb and came to a stop in front of the Peterson Building. The rear window slid noiselessly down to reveal an interior swirling with bluish smoke. A cloud puffed out into the afternoon sunlight like the exhalation of a giant. Salvatore Valestra sat in the backseat, an ascot tucked into the neck of his cashmere overcoat, and a thick cigar clenched in his yellowed teeth.

The driver of the car was a tall, gaunt individual whose dark eyes gleamed with a perpetual nasty leer. He unfolded his length from the front seat and stepped back to open the door for his employer. Valestra emerged scowling into the bright sunlight. He flicked cigar ash onto the sidewalk and stared sourly up at the office building.

Bruce sat uncomfortably in the large swivel chair behind Beaumont's desk, while Beaumont himself smiled down on him from his perch on the edge of the desk top. Andrea stood at her father's side, observing the interaction between the two with a smile of amusement.

Bruce fidgeted slightly in the chair. "I, uh, hope we're not interrupting anything," he said.

"Not at all, not at all," Beaumont assured him. "I'm never too busy for my Andi and her friends." He reached to take his daughter's hand in both of his. "I tell you, Bruce, I do a lot of financial planning.

BATMAN: THE ANIMATED MOVIE

When it comes to money, you can't take the future for granted. But all the money in the world doesn't amount to a thing if you don't have loved ones to share it with. Nothing is more important than family."

Bruce produced a dutiful nod. "Yes, Mr. Beaumont."

"Now, call me Carl," Beaumont insisted with a paternal smile. Just then his speakerphone emitted a short bleat. "Excuse me, sir." His secretary's voice had an anxious edge to it. "But there's a Mr. Valestra here to see you."

Beaumont's smile vanished as his head came up sharply. When he turned toward the door, he had an almost frightened expression on his refined features.

"The gentleman says that he has an appointment," the voice from the speakerphone continued, "but the schedule book doesn't—"

At that moment, Valestra himself swaggered into the office. Beaumont cleared his throat loudly and leaned down toward the speakerphone. "If Mr. Valestra says he has an appointment, Virginia, then Mr. Valestra has an appointment."

Bruce looked from Beaumont to the newcomer as Valestra crossed the floor. The businessman hopped off the desk, a cowed look on his face as the mobster approached him. Valestra took Beaumont's place on the edge of the large desk. He flipped open a carved wooden humidor and helped himself to an expensive cigar.

"That's what I like about your pop, kiddo." Valestra flashed a wide, predatory grin at Andrea as he cupped his hands around a match. His cheeks hollowed, then swelled again as he emitted a cloud of thick smoke. "He's got his priorities in order. . . ."

Two minutes later, Bruce and Andrea emerged from the front door of the Peterson Building. Bruce put his hands in his pockets as they walked out into the sunlight and shuddered. "Is my shirt too big," he said, "or is that just my skin crawling?"

"I hear Mr. Valestra has that effect on people sometimes." Andrea wore an expression of distaste. They turned right and started to walk toward the nearby intersection and the arching bridge beyond it. The long black sedan was still parked at the curb.

The tall driver was standing outside the car, bending forward at the waist to get a close look at his reflection in the mirror on the passenger side. He wet the tip of his index finger and rubbed at something at the corner of his mouth with a small frown. Then his dark eyes widened appreciatively as he caught sight of Andrea coming up behind him. He angled the mirror to watch her approach, then straightened to his full height and gave her a provocative leer as she and Bruce came alongside the car. He pursed his lips in a low wolf whistle as the couple walked past.

Andrea kept her eyes on the bridge ahead of them, but Bruce snapped his head around at the sound of the whistle and scowled in the tall man's direction. The driver curled his thin lips and returned the scowl.

Andrea looked up, catching the exchange. She tugged at his sleeve. "C'mon, Bruce. Dad just counts their money for them. They don't tell him where it comes from."

"It's not your father, Andi—" A trio of low-slung

BATMAN: THE ANIMATED MOVIE

motorcycles roared past, heading for the bridge. Bruce waited for the noise to diminish before continuing. He gestured to the teeming city around them, his scowl becoming a frown of deep concern. "It's the way things are in general . . . it's everything."

As if on cue, a snarl of rage came from up ahead. Bruce and Andrea stopped walking.

A small guardhouse covered with spray-painted graffiti stood at the base of the arching bridge. In front of the guardhouse a street vendor had set up business, hawking hand-crafted jewelry and trinkets from a card table draped with a length of faded blue velvet. The vendor was a small, round man, wearing a green base-ball cap and a brightly patterned sweater. A small peddler's license framed in cracked plastic was pinned to the front of the sweater.

The three men who surrounded him were uniformly tall, burly, and clad in black leather. The closest of the toughs had blond hair pulled back into a greasy po-nytail. He had left his motorcycle and now stood di-rectly in front of the flimsy table, an angry sneer on his stubbly face. His two confederates sat straddling their bikes a short distance away.

As Bruce and Andrea watched, the little man ner-vously scooped money and jewelry from the table and dropped it into a rectangular metal box. He snapped the lid closed and started to back away, the cash box clutched to his chest.

The biker reached out and pried the box loose with one meaty paw. "I *said,* hand over the money, man!" he growled. The vendor grabbed the end of the box as it slipped through his arms, and began a valiant tug-of-war with his much larger adversary.

The biker was obviously not a patient man. He shook the smaller man like a terrier with a mouse. *"Gimme,"* he snarled, "or so help me, I'll mess up your fat face so bad you'll be breathin' outta the part in yer hair!" The other two toughs walked their bikes around behind the little man, effectively surrounding him as the blond man pushed him backward. One of them, a black man with a shaved head, dismounted from his bike and tapped the kickstand down with his heel. He searched inside his jacket and pulled out a wicked-looking blackjack. He started toward the vendor with a menacing look on his scarred face. The third man had red hair combed into a thicket of upstanding spikes. He leaned back against his seat and grinned, a gold tooth shining at the corner of his mouth.

Bruce's hands tightened into fists. He peeled off his jacket, then reached up and loosened his tie. He motioned Andrea behind him. "Stay put," he told her. "This could get serious."

"Bruce, *no!*" She clutched at his arm as he started forward. "Don't!"

He pulled away, staring back at her in amazement. "What do you expect me to do—just stand here?"

Andrea looked at his grim expression and let her hand drop back to her side. "Just come back to me in one piece," she said anxiously. "Please."

The biker with the shaved head came up behind the struggling vendor. Wielding his blackjack almost negligently, he smacked the small man across the back of

BATMAN: THE ANIMATED MOVIE

his baseball cap. The vendor slumped forward with a grunt and collapsed onto his card table, the cash box sliding out of his hands. The flimsy table flattened with a crash, trinkets and bits of bright jewelry scattering onto the pavement. The cash box hit the ground heavily, its lid jarring open with the impact. The blond biker stooped down with a chuckle and caught up the cash box, then straightened with a grunt of surprise as he spotted Bruce, who was charging toward him like a linebacker.

Bruce led with his shoulder, smashing into the ponytailed biker's chest and jarring the box from his grasp. Bruce twisted expertly as the box hit the pavement again and grabbed the other man's jacket. He used a judo flip to toss the biker through the air. The man toppled over a nearby metal railing and plunged into the river with a hoarse yell.

"Man—you are *dead* now!" The second biker punched his fist into a massive palm as he stalked toward Bruce. A motor revved. Out of the corner of his eye, Bruce could see the red-haired tough start up his cycle and move toward him from the other side. A grim smile played on his lips as he settled into a fighting stance, all of his concentration coming to bear on the task at hand. He brought his extensive martial arts training to the forefront of his mind, narrowing the focus of his perceptions to the relaxed, steady beat of his heart. He was the water, wearing away at the boulder drop by drop; the bird carrying off a mountain, one pebble at a time. Three foes or three thousand—it made no difference when one's concentration was total.

Except—

Bruce's serene gaze flickered like a candle caught in a sudden breeze as he glanced to one side. Andrea stood some distance behind him, her hand at her mouth. When Bruce returned his eyes to the two men who were stalking him, a small portion of his concentration wavered, remembering the stricken look on her face. *Just come back to me in one piece,* she had pleaded. His breathing grew ragged and his heartbeat increased in tempo as the two toughs sidled toward him.

The man with the shaved head produced a six-inch switchblade from inside his jacket. He snapped it open with an ugly grin. The one with the red spikes had taken a tire chain from the back of his bike and looped it around his hand several times. His grin flashed with gold. "Hope you got yer insurance all paid up, sucker!" He revved his motor.

Behind Bruce, Andrea watched the display of weapons with growing terror. She jammed her knuckle into her mouth to keep from crying out.

Suddenly the red-haired biker stepped on the gas and shot toward Bruce. Instinctively, Bruce leaped into the air and delivered a pinwheeling roundhouse kick, knocking the chain out of the man's hand as he zoomed past. As Bruce regained his balance, he saw that Andrea had run forward a few paces, putting her dangerously close to the action. His concentration flagged. The black biker hurled himself toward Bruce in a clumsy flying side kick that hit Bruce in the midsection before he could dodge. Bruce managed to lash out with a stiffened hand, knocking the switchblade

BATMAN: THE ANIMATED MOVIE

from the other man's fingers. The knife went skittering along the pavement as Bruce slammed into the guardhouse wall, taking the impact solidly across his shoulder blades.

The red-haired man had wheeled back into the action. He snatched the cash box from the ground with a triumphant cry. As Bruce got swaying to his feet, the shaven-headed man ran to his bike and climbed on board. He kick-started his motor and took off. Bruce charged groggily after the two. He launched himself at the gold-toothed man, just missing him, and landed in a heap on the ground. The two roared onto the arching bridge. The red-haired man gave a hoot of victory, hefting the cash box into the air as he zoomed up and out of sight.

Andrea rushed to Bruce's side, dropping to one knee beside him as he groaned into a sitting position. "Thank god, you're all right!" Her face was white. "I was so frightened."

Bruce made no response. He was seething with anger, most of it directed at himself. Andrea reached out to touch the deep bruise on his cheek. "C'mon, let me have a look at you—"

"Andrea, *please* . . ." Bruce brushed her fingers away with a grunt of annoyance. He scrambled to his feet and moved away from her, stifling a groan of pain. Behind him, Andrea got slowly to her feet. She stood watching him with a mixture of worry and puzzlement.

Later that night, Bruce sat at the desk in his study at Wayne Manor, a drawing pad in front of him. He

MASK OF THE PHANTASM

was sketching in the outline of an amateurish figure, standing in a skin-tight black uniform with a long, flowing cape pinned at the shoulders. He sat back and studied the drawing with a frown, then set down the pencil and turned to stare out the window with a brooding expression. His brow furrowed with disgust. He was on the right track, but there was something lacking. . . . He ripped the drawing from the page and crumpled it up. "What am I still doing this for?" he asked under his breath.

He tossed the wad of paper across the rug and into the blazing hearth.

Alfred appeared in the doorway behind him. The butler took a step forward, then halted as Bruce pounded the arm of his chair. "It's gotta be one way or the other," the young man continued in a fierce whisper. "I can't have it both ways. I can't put my life on the line when there's someone waiting for me to come home."

Alfred cleared his throat delicately and advanced into the room. "Miss Beaumont would be most happy to know that you feel that way, Master Bruce."

Bruce's head shot up in startlement. The butler walked to a nearby end table and picked up the receiver of the telephone extension that sat there. A small red light was flashing steadily. Alfred extended the receiver toward his employer. "She's holding on line one, sir."

Bruce stared at the phone almost fearfully. "Alfred, I can't," he said finally. "Not now." He got to his feet and grabbed his jacket from the back of his chair. He crossed the room and headed out of the study.

BATMAN: THE ANIMATED MOVIE

"But, Master Bruce." Alfred pursed his lips in concern. "What shall I say?"

"I don't know," Bruce called back past his shoulder. "I just don't *know*!" He pounded the edge of the doorway with his palm as he rushed by, then slammed the door shut behind him. The room reverberated with the sound. Alfred touched the small red button and raised the receiver to his ear, a look of sadness passing over his prim features.

Bruce chose a black sports car from the small fleet in the Wayne Manor garage. He drove for half an hour without a destination, then made a decision and headed off down a twisting side road. Fifteen minutes later, he was standing before the tall granite monument inscribed with the names of Thomas and Martha Wayne.

Lightning flashed and thunder sounded a distant counterpoint. He pulled the collar of his light jacket up around his throat as rain began to come down in large, cold drops. He stood staring at the towering monument, oblivious of the mounting downpour, an expression of pleading on his face.

"It doesn't mean I don't care anymore," he said softly to the night. "I *don't* want to let you down, honestly. But—" He winced as a bright flash of lightning illuminated the cemetery. Thunder rolled above his head. "It's just that—it doesn't hurt so bad anymore. You can understand that, can't you?" He shook his head, as if aware that his argument lacked conviction. "Look, I can give money to the city; they can hire more cops. Let someone else take the risks. It's different now." His voice grew softer but at the same time more urgent. "*Please.* I need it to be different now."

Bruce's rain-streaked face was a battleground of conflicting emotions. He sank slowly to his knees in the mud and grass, clasping his hands in front of him. "I know I made a promise, but I didn't see this coming. I didn't count on being happy."

His eyes reflected an infinite longing as he leaned forward, clutching the base of the large monument as if he were gripping someone's shoulders. "Please," he whispered. "Tell me that it's okay. . . ."

Wind lashed at the branches of nearby trees, sending a shower of dark leaves to mingle with the downpour. Then a voice came out of the darkness behind him: "Maybe they already have."

Bruce whirled around, his eyes wide. Andrea stood several yards away, a slight, dark silhouette beneath a drooping umbrella. She stepped toward him out of the shadows. "Maybe they sent *me*."

Bruce rose unsteadily to his feet. His pants were soaked and muddy and he shivered in the chill wind. Andrea came into his arms and he turned his face toward the darkness as he held her.

Batman clung to his perch on the cathedral ledge as his thoughts returned to the present. Rain poured down, dripping steadily from his cape and cowl. He heard a lazy rumbling sound and turned his face upward. A large police blimp was drifting overhead, its searchlights slicing down through the curtains of rain

BATMAN: THE ANIMATED MOVIE

to sweep the dark streets far below. As it passed above the cathedral, one of its beams flashed over the spot near the gargoyle where the Dark Knight had been crouching.

It was empty.

NINETEEN

The next morning brought sunshine and blue skies to Gotham. Councilman Arthur Reeves had decided to walk to work, enjoying the cool breeze and the tangy smell of fall in the air. He came briskly down the sidewalk, whistling cheerfully as he overtook other pedestrians, and stepping nimbly around the puddles left from the night before. His campaign against Batman was proceeding nicely, with public opinion mounting in his favor. If Gordon continued to be stubborn, Reeves would soon have him exactly where he wanted him: out of office. Life would be considerably easier if the next commissioner were more familiar with the view from Reeves's pocket. With Gordon gone and the Dark Knight on the run from the law, there was no telling what he could accomplish in this town. The councilman smiled broadly. He could tell it was going to be a good day.

As he started to cross the mouth of a narrow alleyway, a long black limousine nosed suddenly into view,

BATMAN: THE ANIMATED MOVIE

blocking the sidewalk. Reeves caught sight of his own reflection in the mirrored windows and stepped back, startled. The rear window slid down.

"Get in," Sal Valestra said to him, his hoarse voice little more than a rough whisper. He raised a skeletal thumb and jabbed it in the direction of the empty seat at his side. "Now."

The sight of the frail old man on a busy street in broad daylight sent a shock through Arthur Reeves. He paused, making sure no one was watching him, then circled around to the other side of the limo and crawled quickly into the backseat. Valestra sat crumpled against the far door like a discarded rag doll. A pair of oxygen tanks, one of them fitted with a yellowed plastic mask, sat on the seat between them. Valestra raised a withered arm and signaled through the glass partition to the driver, a young woman with close-cropped blond hair. "Drive."

As the car pulled smoothly out and joined the flow of traffic, Valestra leaned around the metal cylinders and scowled at Reeves.

"All I want to know is, is it true?" he rasped. "Is the Batman really hitting our people?"

"Indisputably." Reeves gave a grim nod. "There were eyewitnesses in both cases."

"Beautiful. That's just beautiful." Valestra's shrunken features contorted into a mask of fury. "Why is he doing this? He never leaned on us before." He gave a rheumy cough and settled back against the seat cushion. "I'm too old for this kinda stunt!"

Reeves looked at the other man with a mixture of

pity and disgust. "I suppose you could demand police protection if you're really worried," he said.

Valestra's head jerked around the oxygen tanks to stare at him. "What are you, a comedian? This is *Batman* we're talking about here." Spittle formed a pale froth at the corners of his mouth as he began to gasp for breath. "That freak'll stop at nothing—he'll—crucify me—"

The old man's words were drowned in a series of racking, wheezing coughs. He lunged forward to scrabble at the nearest tank, jerking the mask free and clutching it to his face. With his free hand he twisted frantically at the valve on the top of the cylinder, until a faint hiss began. His sunken cheeks belled and sagged rhythmically as he sucked hungrily at the oxygen.

Reeves suppressed a shudder. He leaned forward to rap sharply on the partition. "Pull over," he ordered, watching Valestra from the corner of his eye. "It's not very healthy in here."

TWENTY

Batman sat at the main computer station in the Batcave, inputting data with rapid strokes of the keyboard. He punched Enter, then sat back and scanned the screen as words began to appear in glowing lines.

"O'Neil Funding Corporation . . . Adams Tool and Die . . . Resnick Sand Blasting . . ." He nodded slowly as the list of names filled the screen. "I should have known."

"Sir?" Alfred held up the fencing foil he was polishing and squinted along its gleaming length in the light from the big computer screen. Satisfied, he returned it to its place on the wall rack and walked to stand behind Batman's chair at the console.

"Chuckie Sol and Buzz Bronski." The Dark Knight tipped his chin up at the screen. "It appears they have some history together." He touched a key and the screen cleared. A second list appeared. "They were partners in several dummy corporations set up more than ten years ago.''

Alfred folded the rectangle of cloth he had been using and draped it carefully on the edge of the console. ''Interesting,'' he said. ''And now both have met an untimely death within mere days of one another.''

A bar of light was moving slowly down the screen, highlighting a roster of names. It held on the last name and pulsed silently. ''It turns out there were actually three men involved in this partnership,'' Batman said. He nodded at the blinking line. ''The third director in each of these enterprises was one Salvatore Valestra, reputed mob boss.'' He paused, then gave another slow nod, a glint of recognition in the dark eyes behind the mask. ''Valestra.''

He rose from the console and turned to Alfred. ''Sal's having company tonight,'' he told the butler. ''No need to wait up.'' He strode off toward the Batmobile, which waited silently on its massive turntable, a gleam of black curves in the dim light.

Alfred watched his employer go with a hopeful expression. ''Meaning, I trust, that once you've concluded your business with Mr. Valestra, you'll be seeing _her_?''

The Dark Knight froze at the cockpit of the sleek vehicle. ''You think you know everything about me, don't you?'' he asked without turning, his tone defiant.

Alfred folded his arms across his chest, a hint of irritation creeping into his own demeanor. ''I used to diaper your bottom—I bloody well ought to.'' He pursed his lips as Batman shot him a sharp look. *"Sir."*

The masked man lowered himself into the cockpit. "Well, you're wrong," he said coldly as the canopy began to slide shut above him. He started the vehicle and slammed his boot down on the gas pedal. The afterburner flared like a comet's tail and the Batmobile roared off.

Alfred heaved a troubled sigh and returned to the rack of swords.

The Dark Knight left the Batmobile parked in the shadows of a littered alley behind Sal Valestra's town house. He gained entrance via his grapple gun and an unlocked upstairs window. Valestra's study still smelled of the cigars its owner had been forbidden to smoke for almost a decade. Batman shuffled through the pile of bank statements and personal papers strewn over the surface of the huge desk. A gleam glimpsed from the corner of his eye caused him to shift the beam of his tiny flashlight to the wall.

Sal Valestra himself, in various stages of decay, leered from a double row of glossy photographs, the top ones mostly colored and the lower ones black and white. The Dark Knight clicked on the gooseneck lamp on the desk and tilted its shade upward to provide more light.

There was Valestra looking jovial, his arm around the padded shoulders of a well-known nightclub singer; and there he stood winking suggestively at an actress famed for her weakness for boyfriends with unsavory pasts. To the right of that photo, Valestra

MASK OF THE PHANTASM

stood with a shovel in his hand and a look of determination on his thin face, at the forefront of a line of union workers. The Dark Knight's lip curled as his beam traveled over a large picture of Gotham City's current mayor, who smiled weakly into the camera as he and reputed underworld figure Sal Valestra stood before a dilapidated housing project. Valestra's arm was draped in comradely fashion across the mayor's shoulder, and the camera had almost managed to capture the latter's unconscious wince.

A series of pictures followed featuring a rogues gallery of Gotham's other celebrated gangsters: Valestra was seen consorting with a weary-looking Arnold Stromwell and a dapper Rupert Thorne, while Roland Daggett's broad smile and calculating eyes loomed over the head of the smaller Valestra in a gilt-framed 8 × 10 that was obviously considered one of the gems of the retired mobster's collection.

Finally the pencil-beam halted on a somewhat faded photo of four men in a booth at an expensive-looking restaurant. Champagne was being lifted in a toast by the smiling quartet, and the Dark Knight's beam lingered in turn on the faces of the celebrants: Buzz Bronski, Chuckie Sol, Sal Valestra. . . . The tall figure of Valestra's chauffeur lurked in the shadows just behind the fourth member of the happy group: Carl Beaumont.

Behind the mask, Batman's eyes narrowed. He stared at the self-satisfied grin on Beaumont's face as his thoughts traveled back to another place and time. . . .

* * *

BATMAN: THE ANIMATED MOVIE

The sky above them was overcast, an expanse of slate-gray striations that grew progressively darker and more threatening as the sun sank into the west, sending up golden shafts like searchlight beams before it disappeared entirely from view.

Bruce and Andrea strolled along a rough path near the edge of the high, rocky promontory that marked the end of Bruce's property far to the rear of Wayne Manor. On one side of them the tiny yellow lights of the mansion could be seen above the sloping grounds; on the other, surf pounded and withdrew relentlessly along a border of jagged rocks far below.

"You know how much I've always wanted to see Europe," Andrea was saying as they walked. Bruce was conscious of the warmth of her palm against his own. "And Dad has business there beginning next week—some sort of hush-hush deal. He won't tell me a thing." She paused to take a deep breath, then continued, her eyes on the grassy trail. "He can't even say when we'd be coming back."

Bruce stood still, looking down at Andrea. He cleared his throat. As always, little of what he was feeling showed on his face. "Will you at least let me *try* to talk you out of this?" His voice had developed a slight tremble, hinting at the depth of the dismay he was feeling. He put an arm around her shoulders and steered her off the path. He brought her to a broad, smooth rock that jutted up at the edge of a narrow crevice in the earth.

"Bruce . . ."

"Wait." He pressed down gently on her shoulder, guiding her to a seat on the rock. "Please?" He gazed down at her blankly for a few heartbeats, feeling like an actor who has forgotten his lines. Finally he heaved a gusty sigh. "Oh, look, I'm no good at this." He rummaged in the inside pocket of his jacket and pulled out a tiny velvet box. He held it in his palm and stared down at it, almost in surprise, then he knelt by the side of the rock and handed it to her. "Here, open it. You'll get the idea."

Andrea cradled the box in her palms, then lifted the lid in silence. The ring was beautiful, the diamond glittering with cold fire in the last rays of the sun. "Oh, Bruce . . ."

"Well." He felt the pull of unfamiliar muscles on his face. I must be grinning like a fool, he thought with a touch of embarrassment. He dismissed the thought, defiance replacing the disapproval. So what? Maybe acting like a fool once in a while wasn't such a bad thing, after all. He beamed down at her, his throat suddenly dry. "What do you say?" he croaked.

"Of course I will." There was a faraway roaring in the night air, a rhythmic sound that Bruce at first took to be the blood pounding in his ears. He held the box for her as she removed the ring and slipped it onto her finger.

She lifted it wonderingly, a transient sparkle in the dim light. "I never thought this would actually happen." Her voice was hushed. "I always felt like . . . like something completely unexpected in your life, that you never knew quite what to do with. . . ." She looked up into his eyes. "Because I wasn't part of your plan."

"You are now," Bruce told her huskily. He leaned

forward and gathered her into his arms. "I'm changing the plan."

The roaring sound had grown louder as they spoke. Suddenly the crevice at their feet erupted with an explosion of black wings, as hundreds of small flying things burst out into the night.

"What—" Bruce threw a protective arm in front of Andrea's face and pulled her to her feet. Stunned, the two staggered back from the opening. Heart pounding in his throat, Bruce guided Andrea to a small stand of stunted trees not far from the cliff's edge. They looked up in awe as the bats kept coming, swirling above the crevice in a great vortex till they blanketed the darkening sky. Bruce held her in his arms and shook his head in wonder while they clung together. "Quite a sight, isn't it?"

"I wouldn't exactly call it a good omen," Andrea said ruefully. She managed a shaky smile as he drew her closer. "I've always been a little bit afraid of bats. . . ."

An hour later, the Wayne limousine pulled into the long suburban driveway of the Beaumont mansion, its tires crunching on white stones as it made its way down the circular drive before the front door. Two cars were already parked there ahead of them.

Andrea and Bruce sat in the back, with Alfred ramrod straight in his livery behind the wheel. Andrea was wearing Bruce's jacket draped over her shoulders. She frowned when she noticed the lighted window in the east wing of the ground floor. The silhouettes of several individuals were visible through the drawn curtains, one seated behind a desk, the others facing him.

"Uh oh." Andrea's frown grew puzzled. "Looks like Dad's got company. Business-type company. He almost never sees clients at home." She glanced down at the band of silver on her slim wrist. "Especially not at this hour."

Bruce got out of the limo, crossed around the back, and came up to open Andrea's door for her. She stepped out and the two moved close to each other. "Maybe this isn't the best time for our announcement." Andrea glanced back at the lighted window and bit her lip. "Maybe we'd better wait till tomorrow to give him the good news."

Bruce shrugged. "Whatever you think is best." He lifted his jacket from her shoulders. There was a beat of silence before they moved together in a kiss. Bruce looked down into her face intently, as if trying to commit her features to memory. "Good night."

"Good night, Bruce." She leaned down to smile across the front seat. "Alfred."

"Miss Beaumont." The butler inclined his head.

She headed up the steps to the front porch, a thoughtful expression on her face. A tall man leaned against a column at the top of the steps, a black fedora pulled low on his narrow brow. A cigarette hung from his wide mouth. He was poking at his cuticles with a fingernail file. Andrea looked past him as she strode purposefully into the house. The tall man gave her an appreciative leer, making a low growling noise deep in his throat. He took a long, last drag on his cigarette as she entered the front door, then turned his attention to the limousine pulling slowly away in the drive. Bruce watched in open hostility from the back window as the tall man flicked the still-burning butt in the limo's direction, his wide grin altering to a sneer of contempt. The cigarette bounced off the polished side of the car as it headed away from the house.

Bruce's brow knit in a frown of recognition. Surely he had seen this obnoxious man before. He remembered the driver who had been admiring himself in the side mirror of Sal Valestra's car outside Beaumont's office building. His frown deepened.

The top six inches of a painter's ladder were visible above the rough lip of the crevice. Beyond, the surf rolled unseen on the other side of the towering promontory.

"It's another cave, all right." The muffled voice came from inside the crevice. "Could be as big as the house." A flashlight beam played up over the tip of the ladder, then a strong hand gripped the wooden rung and Bruce pulled himself into view. He was dressed in old jeans and a sweatshirt with HOKKAIDO UNIVERSITY emblazoned in orange across the front. There was a thoughtful look on his face as he squatted at the edge of the opening. "Judging from the number of bats that came pouring out of it last night, it could be as big as Gotham Stadium. . . ." He blinked up into the brightness. Alfred was standing silently not far from the crevice, the mid-morning sun behind his back. His face was a study in controlled dismay. Bruce inspected him curiously as his eyes adjusted gradually to the glare.

MASK OF THE PHANTASM

"Alfred? What's wrong?"

The butler held out his right hand. In his palm lay a tiny package wrapped in brown paper. He handed it to Bruce. "This just arrived with the morning post, sir." His voice was subdued.

Bruce took the package and rose to his feet, staring down at it in bafflement. He tore the paper away to reveal the black velvet of the ring box. Taped to the top of the box was a folded letter.

Bruce opened the note and scanned it, muttering softly under his breath as he read.

" 'Dear Bruce . . . left with Dad . . . too young . . . need time . . . forget about me . . . ?' "

His fingers contracted around the letter, crumpling it into a tiny ball. The wad of paper slipped from his slackening hand and tumbled down into the black crevice as his face contorted in sudden grief.

The young man stood motionless for the space of several heartbeats. In his mind's eye he saw the portrait of his parents that had hung for years in the study of the mansion. Thomas and Martha stood stiffly erect, formal and unsmiling, their eyes seeming to say, *We told you . . .*

The image dissolved in his mind to become the blackness of the crevice, descending endlessly into the cold earth.

Alfred turned his face away as his young master threw back his head and cried out in anguish.

Stalactites dripped cloudy limestone tears. Rough cavern walls rose into rustling darkness. A faint shaft of evening light penetrated the gloom from far above.

BATMAN: THE ANIMATED MOVIE

A candle sat on a natural shelf jutting from the rock walls, providing a wan glow. Within the pale circle of light sat a metal table, two chairs, and a gleaming new computer terminal.

Alfred Pennyworth stood just within the candle's glow and gazed somberly into the greater darkness beyond. Over his hand was draped something that resembled a hood and cowl of stiff black fabric. The whisper of leathery wings came from above. A softer sound issued from just outside the circle of light, where slow, methodical movements revealed a man drawing on a form-fitting uniform and adjusting a pair of black gloves. His back was to the older man, his silhouette blurred by a long cloak. As Alfred watched, he lifted a gleaming golden belt from the table and fitted it carefully around his waist, fumbling just a bit with the complicated clasp. Then, without turning, he held out his hand to the other man. Alfred swallowed and moved forward, doubt in his eyes. He transferred the hoodlike object to the outstretched hand and stepped back.

The man in the shadows gripped the mask in both his hands, staring grimly at it for a long moment. Then he bowed his head and drew it slowly on. He inhaled deeply and turned around.

Alfred took an involuntary step backward, his mouth opening soundlessly.

Gone was the boy he had cared for from childhood, the young man he had watched over, both as servant and substitute parent. Standing before him in Bruce Wayne's place was a creature dark and terrible, a silent, menacing *thing* whose eyes glowed with a cold determined flame.

A black cloak with edges scalloped like the wings of a bat hung almost to the floor over the form-fitting gray suit. The image of a bat in flight was drawn in black upon the costume's chest, and the grim motif was repeated in the mask and cowl, which rose in two sharp points above the man's head. The butler retreated another step, edging toward the lone candle as the black-garbed figure moved in his direction. "My god," Alfred whispered. He turned to stare as the transformed man moved silently past him, disappearing into the shadows of the cavern as if he were a part of them.

The Dark Knight gave his cowled head a small shake as his thoughts returned to the present. He was standing in the study of Sal Valestra's town house, staring down at the photograph he had lifted from the wall. He scanned the faces at the restaurant table once more: Bronski, Sol, Valestra, Beaumont. Three had been living in Gotham until recently. Now two of those were dead. One had left the city a decade ago and stayed away; his current whereabouts were unknown.

Batman slipped the photo beneath his cape and melted into the darkness.

TWENTY-ONE

The moon shone an antique ivory light on the site of the Gotham World's Fair, casting long shadows from the abandoned buildings and time-worn exhibits.

Headlights probed the main entrance. A rusted chain lay useless on the highway, allowing the long black limousine to pass unhindered into the deserted landscape of fantasy and dreams. The car slowed as it reached a sizable intersection, took a sharp left at Science Land, and made its way down the unlit thoroughfares toward the shining domes and towers of the Forward to the Future exhibit.

The limo came to a quiet halt at the base of an upward spiraling ramp. Half a dozen sawhorse barriers had been arranged haphazardly in front of the sagging walkway.

The headlights snapped off.

After a moment the rear door of the limo creaked open and a fragile-looking Salvatore Valestra crawled

MASK OF THE PHANTASM

out into the moonlight. He paused and considered the expanse of deserted fairgrounds, his thin shoulders slumping under a trench coat three sizes too large. He carried a battered briefcase in his left hand and a portable oxygen bottle in his right. He set down the briefcase and raised the bottle to his face, inhaling deeply through the attached mask. He lowered the bottle after a few seconds, his face grayish. "If only there were some other way," he muttered to himself. Then he squared his frail shoulders. Picking up the briefcase, he walked past the sawhorses and started up the ramp.

Something stirred in the shadows of a nearby archway as Valestra mounted the gently sloping walkway. A dark shape in a long black cloak watched intently for several moments, then melted back into the darkness.

The old mobster was breathing heavily by the time he stepped from the top of the ramp onto the horizontal skywalk that ran from the Life Sciences Museum to the Forward to the Future pavilion. Valestra headed toward the entranceway of the latter building, his eyes on the arching doorways and the four robots, each twice the height of a man, who sat impassively with their metal legs dangling in the moonlight. Rust and decay had worked on their once-gleaming exteriors. Now they seemed like scarred survivors of an ancient war. Each mechanical man had his left arm raised in an attitude of triumphant welcome. Valestra smiled wanly at the empty gesture.

A recessed track bisected the pavement in front of the seated robots. A line of empty cars waited to carry visitors into the wonders of tomorrow. The old man edged between two of the silent conveyances and walked toward the entrance, his breathing labored. He had stopped for a quick pull on the oxygen bottle when he heard a sharp clicking noise from somewhere inside the pavilion.

At once, brightly colored lights flashed on above him. Valestra stared up at them uncomprehendingly, as tinny music issued from the archways, the melodies sounding thin and wavering at first, then growing slowly stronger. Above the doorways, the four robots jerked to life. Lowering their welcoming hands, they began to sway spasmodically back and forth, their heavy metal jaws bobbing grotesquely up and down. Legs swung stiffly and arms moved in unison as a quavering, badly pitched version of the ride's theme song began to play:

> Forward, Gotham, to the future,
> Our dreams are shining bright.
> Glory and wonder—

The staccato of machine-gun fire sounded over the quavering music. Valestra staggered back in horror as bullets riddled the head and torso of the robot on his far left, shattering its outer shell and reducing it to a sparking hulk of exposed electron tubes and fizzing wires.

The old mobster turned to run, lost his balance, and sprawled heavily on the pavement. He rolled over onto his stomach and cowered facedown, his hands clasped at the back of his head. Above him, the gunfire traveled lazily over the remaining dolls, demolish-

MASK OF THE PHANTASM

ing their smiling heads one by one till the decapitated quartet hung limply above the entrance, a gruesome tableau that still twitched erratically to the distorted music.

Then the song was abruptly cut off. Valestra waited for a few moments in the silence. As he raised his eyes fearfully, a tiny foot-long autogyro buzzed by overhead. He stared up at it curiously, then turned his gaze to the pavilion.

A tall, thin shape leaned indolently in the shadows of a side doorway, its own head lost in darkness. With a soft chuckle, the figure stepped forward, its face wreathed for an instant in the bluish smoke rising from the mouth of the machine gun. Valestra cringed. He had forgotten how unnerving this sight could be.

The first thing he saw was the first thing anyone saw: the hideously elongated frozen smile. Then the eyes, rimmed in black, staring, malevolent. The skin of the face had the unnatural pallor of a corpse, the perfect background for the startling scarlet of the lips. The head itself was long and narrow under its cap of dark mossy green hair, its jaw jutting obscenely beneath the horrible grin.

The Joker tossed his machine gun to one side. "I hate that song," he said matter-of-factly.

TWENTY-TWO

Valestra's breath came in shuddery gasps as he struggled to push himself up on thin elbows. His oxygen bottle and briefcase lay on the cracked pavement beside him.

The clown-faced creature left the doorway and walked toward the old mobster, his frozen grin contorted into a parody of concern. Halfway to the old man's side, he stopped and slapped his gloved palms to the sides of his face in comic astonishment.

"Gasp!" he said. "Can it *be*?" He folded his white-gloved hands against his long chin and batted his eyelashes at the fallen mobster like a cartoon schoolgirl. "Old Sallie 'the Wheezer' Valestra, here on my doorstep!" He rushed forward as the old man managed to totter to his feet and clapped him solidly between the shoulders. Valestra reeled under the blow.

"Welcome, *paisan*'!" The Joker gave a hoot of shrill laughter. "It's been a dog's age—and an elderly pooch, at that!"

MASK OF THE PHANTASM

Valestra had gathered up his briefcase and oxygen bottle. He cradled them awkwardly in his arms as the other man embraced him.

The Joker was wearing a purple suit whose long tails flapped in the back. He had a small plastic carnation in his lapel and a green string tie knotted at his throat.

Valestra was conscious of the sweat dripping down inside his collar. "Heh." He cleared his throat and attempted a shaky smile. "Hello, Joker," he rasped, still gasping for breath. "Didn't mean to—disturb you—by dropping by unannounced."

"Sal-va-tor-ay! Why so formal, pray tell?" The clown pulled the old man in for a second comradely hug, then pushed him out to arm's length, knocking the cylinder and the briefcase onto the pavement once more as he gave the other man a rough slap on the back and pumped his hand enthusiastically. *"Mi casa es su casa,"* he announced with a sweeping gesture. He bent to gather up the briefcase and bottle, shoving them back into Valestra's shaking arms. "Getting a little clumsy in our dotage, aren't we?"

He gave the old man yet another shove, reached out, and snagged him by the lapels, yanking him close.

"So—what's an old-timer like you want with a two-timer like me, hmmm?" Another shove sent the old man reeling backward to collide with the nearest car of the little train.

"Uhh, business, Joker. I got business—"

"Ooooh, business!" The Joker's eyebrows waggled. "Sounds like fun, Sallie." The grotesque clown took a short run and leaped across the several feet that separated them. "Come, my broken-down buddy," he said, "let us 'repair' to more comfortable environs. But first—" He squinted hard at the old man, holding one hand high up over his head as if measuring him. "You must be at least this tall to go on this attraction!"

The Joker nodded his head back and forth several times between his white glove and the top of the old man's head. Then he brought his hand down hard, mashing Valestra's hat down over his ears. "Close enough!" he exclaimed. Valestra gave a pained gasp as the clown yanked him up by his collar. The Joker lifted the old mobster into the air and slammed him down into the front seat of the first small car. The bottle and briefcase flew from Valestra's hands to tumble into the seat next to him. As the old man struggled to pry his hat off his head, the Joker grabbed the safety bar and plunged it down onto his dazed passenger's crotch. The old man gasped and curled forward into a fetal position. "Now hold onto those hats and spectacles, please!" the clown sang. He slid his long legs down into the seat next to Valestra. "There's just a *teensy* little bit of a jump at the start. . . ." The Joker yanked on a lever at his side and the car shot forward like a rocket.

"Yiiiiiii!" Valestra wailed uncontrollably until the Joker reached over with a grimace of annoyance and clapped his gloved hand over the old man's mouth. "I *think* what you're trying to say is 'wheeeeeee'!" he told the terrified mobster, as the car zoomed down the track toward the House of the Future. Inside the World of the Future's vast dome, the little train streaked past

MASK OF THE PHANTASM

darkened dioramas depicting the exploration of space and the exploitation of wondrous devices, now crumbling with age and disuse. Space-age appliances, fantastic bubble cars, and personal robots bent in attitudes of subservience zipped by. Valestra closed his eyes and concentrated desperately on his breathing until he felt the car slowing. He peeked cautiously out of one eye.

The home of tomorrow had definitely seen better days.

Dust clung in a soft coat to the recessed light bulbs. Chrome surfaces were pitted and discolored and swatches of futuristic fabric lay in tatters.

The little train screeched to an abrupt halt, sending Valestra flopping forward onto the front of his car. The train shuddered and fell silent. On the right side of the track, the android housewife, its blond-wigged head askew and dappled with rust, stood at a freestanding kitchen counter and chopped mindlessly at the empty countertop with her tarnished knife. Across the track, her husband's couch was ominously vacant, and near it stood a decaying robot dog, his exposed wire tail wagging fitfully.

The Joker put his foot on the top of the car door and leaped gaily onto the worn rug. He landed with a jaunty bow, throwing his arms wide in the direction of the robot housewife.

"Honey, I'm home!" he proclaimed loudly. "Or is that 'Homey, I'm a Hun'?"

Valestra lifted his head, gasping painfully for air. He fumbled frantically for his portable oxygen bottle,

BATMAN: THE ANIMATED MOVIE

located it, and crawled out of the ride behind the Joker.

The ancient mechanical dog had left the side of the couch. It hobbled toward the two men, its wire tail spinning like a propeller and its furless jaw opening and shutting slowly as excited yapping sounds came from somewhere inside its body.

"Rusty!" The Joker snapped his gloved fingers at the decrepit robot as it continued to bark. He looked back at Valestra with a playful twinkle in his black-rimmed eyes. "Oh, don't mind my little home security system. He's really just a harmless pup." He cocked his leg back and gave the small machine a sudden powerful kick. Valestra watched as the robot canine sailed into the air and out through a nearby window of the diorama. Broken glass showered the carpet.

"Out, Rusty!" the Joker called cheerfully, cupping his hand behind his ear to catch the response. A burst of muffled yapping sounded from somewhere behind the plastic walls. "Ah, yes. Android's best friend and a super little watchdog." He tapped the side of his long nose with a white finger. "Can't be too careful with all these weirdos running around loose nowadays," he commented to no one in particular. Valestra slapped the oxygen mask to his face and inhaled in great gulps.

The Joker sidled up to the android homemaker. He stared down in surprise at the empty table beneath its relentlessly chopping blade. "What, meatloaf again?" His grotesque features contorted in exaggerated disappointment. "Aww, baby, I had it for lunch." He flashed a naughty grin over his shoulder to Valestra

MASK OF THE PHANTASM

and reached out to pinch the crumbling plastic cheek. "So, what do you think of the little woman, Sallie? Isn't Hazel here a cutie?" He pursed his scarlet lips judiciously. "True, she's a real homebody, but you can't help who you fall in love with." A piece of pink pseudoflesh came off in the clown's fingertips. He inspected it casually, shrugged, and dropped it into the breast pocket of his purple coat.

The old mobster was standing warily next to the dilapidated sofa. The Joker ambled up to his side and bent in a courtly bow. As he straightened, he shoved Valestra backward, knocking him down onto the dusty cushion. "Have a seat, Sal, ol' pal, and tell me what's on your so-called mind." He lifted the tails of his coat and flopped down comfortably in a creaking futuristic chair. A mechanized footstool trundled obediently over to position itself in front of the clown's pointed black boots. The Joker lifted his feet with a sigh and crossed his ankles on the stool as Valestra perched nervously on the edge of the couch.

"It's Batman," whispered the old man. "He—he's gone nuts." A small cloud of dust puffed upward around him as he settled back against the cushion. He sneezed once and cleared his throat. "First he whacked Chuckie Sol, then he took out Buzz—and now he's after me. I *know* it!" His voice cracked on the verge of hysteria and he started to wheeze. "Coupla days ago I saw him spying on me from the roof across the alley!" He tugged at his collar, jamming the oxygen bottle against his face.

"Hmmm . . ." The Joker reclined in his chair with his long arms crossed behind his head. "Y'know, I've

been reading some very upsetting things about ol'
Guano Man lately. Seems he's wound tight enough to
snap.'' He leaned forward thoughtfully, his fingers
forming a white tent in front of his frozen leer. Then
he gave a sudden loud cackle and wriggled his fingers
at the sides of his cheeks. "Oooh! Oooh! Wouldn't it
be soo-*blime* if I've finally driven Herr Batmeister
right off the deep end?'' He pulled his bony knees up
under his pointed chin with a squeal of infantile
delight.

Valestra watched the clown's antics with an expression of wounded shock. "Hey, this ain't a joke!'' The
old mobster got to his feet with a groan and started to
pace back and forth in front of the sofa. "Batman's
knockin' us off one by one, and you're the only guy
that can take him down.'' Valestra lifted his briefcase
from the couch and fumbled with the latches. He pried
the cover back and displayed the contents to the Joker.
"Look. Five million up front and whatever you want
to finish him off.''

The Joker unfolded his long body from the chair
and strolled over to Valestra's side. He lifted a stack
of thousand-dollar bills from the case, riffled them
with his thumb, and smelled them as if sniffing an im-
ported cigar. He raised a contemptuous eyebrow.
"You're offering *me* money? What do I look like, pest
control?'' He gave a cavernous yawn, fanning the
stack of bills in front of his mouth. Then he tossed
them back into the briefcase.

Valestra's hysteria was mounting. "Think, you
grinning fool!'' The old man flung the briefcase onto
the sofa. It slid off the dusty cushions and dropped

MASK OF THE PHANTASM

onto the floor, spilling half a million in freshly minted bills. "Once he gets me, how long till he comes for you?" He stalked forward and clutched the Joker's lapels. "You know what I'm talking about. *Your* hands are just as dirty as mine—dirtier!"

The Joker's eyes had narrowed into black slits the moment Valestra's hands touched his coat. Now his grin stretched downward into a murderous scowl. He rose to his full height, towering over the old mobster as he broke the feeble grip with a savage swipe of his hand. He grabbed the older man by the wisps of gray hair on the back of his head and thrust his white face close to that of the trembling mobster.

"Don't . . . *touch* . . . me, old man," he snarled as Valestra cringed. Then his mood abruptly shifted. He leaned back, the scarlet lips again pulled back in a wide grin. "After all," he said impishly, "I don't know *where* you've been." He released the mobster and placed a friendly arm around his hunched shoulders. He gave a good-natured laugh. "Oh, Sal-a-man-der. No one could take a joke like you." The clown shook his head and rolled his eyes. "Of *course* I'll help you out."

The only sound in the room was the mechanical chopping of the android housewife. The mobster stared at the bizarre criminal for a long disbelieving moment. "Heh. Really, Joker?" Valestra allowed a note of hope to creep into his voice for the first time.

"Certainement, mon vieux parapluie!" The clown puffed out his chest and hugged the old man solicitously to his bosom. "No way is anybody gonna hurt my ol' pal Sal."

BATMAN: THE ANIMATED MOVIE

Valestra managed a hesitant smile. The Joker pointed a white-gloved finger at the mobster's face with an exclamation of delight. *"That's* it! That's what I want to see!" He prodded at the corners of Valestra's thin lips, then turned his finger back to indicate his own grinning face. "A nice, big smile . . ."

TWENTY-THREE

The blades of the police helicopter thrummed rhythmically in the darkness as the aircraft glided past the roof of the luxury hotel. Batman waited for the copter's landing lights to shrink to pinpoints in the night sky before he rose up from the shadows on the rooftop. He moved to the edge of the roof and vanished over the side, lowering himself on a slender line. He dropped lightly onto the balcony outside the bedroom of a lavish suite three floors down and shook the rope to release it.

He extracted something small and narrow from his utility belt and worked at the lock on the French doors for a few seconds. The door swung inward and he stepped into the darkness. As he was easing the glass panel shut behind him, a key turned in the outer door of the suite. The Dark Knight crossed quickly into the shadows at the back of the bedroom.

The door opened and Andrea Beaumont stood silhouetted in the light from the hallway. "I'm exhausted," she said. "Thanks again for dinner, Artie."

Arthur Reeves moved into view behind her. "You know, it's not healthy to go to bed on a full stomach." His fingers strayed down to stroke her hand where it rested on the door handle. "I hear conversation's good for the digestion. Maybe we could stay up and talk for a little while . . ."

"Oh, Artie . . ." Andrea stifled a yawn, turning away as he brought his face closer to hers. Her eyes darted around the interior of the suite as she tried to think of a graceful way to end the evening early. "I've got a real killer of a day tomorrow," she said. "The banks, the attorney . . ." She stiffened as her eyes caught a hint of movement through the doorway of her bedroom. The door to the balcony was standing slightly open, its long white curtain billowing in the breeze from outside. Her eyes widened. Reeves noticed her distraction and stepped in past her, trying to see what had caught her attention. She took his arm and smiled, lifting her other hand to turn his face back to hers.

"But call me, okay?" She leaned forward and gave him a quick kiss on the lips.

Batman watched impassively from the shadows of the bedroom as the councilman reacted in pleased surprise. Then Andrea was ushering him back out into the hallway. "Good night, Artie."

"Uh, yeah—night." Reeves looked slightly confused as she shut the door firmly behind him. Andrea leaned back against the door with a sigh of relief. Then she straightened her shoulders. She walked to the bedroom doorway, stepped inside, and flicked on a lamp.

Batman stood revealed in his hiding place against the blue brocaded wallpaper. Andrea approached him. She stopped a few feet away and surveyed him coolly, hands on hips.

"Don't you ever knock?" she asked. She crossed the room and sat down on a small bench at the foot of the bed. She removed her high heels and began to massage her right foot with an air of nonchalance.

Batman's heart was pounding at the top of his throat. He stepped away from the wall and reached into his cape. Then he lifted the glossy black-and-white photograph into the light. "Have you ever seen this before?" he asked.

A chill feathered Andrea's spine at the husky whisper of his voice. She took the picture from his black-gloved hand and studied it. Then she shook her head. "No," she told him in an uninterested voice. "Never."

"But that's your father, sitting there with Sol, Bronski, and Valestra." Batman tilted his head and gave her a quizzical glance. "I did some checking. He's the one who set up a corporate partnership for them ten years ago."

"So?" Andrea shrugged as she got to her feet. She moved away from him to stand before her dresser. "That was his job."

"He was the one element that tied these three gangsters together," the Dark Knight persisted. "Where's your father now?"

Andrea moved from the dresser to a small teak bar

BATMAN: THE ANIMATED MOVIE

in a corner of the room. She lifted the top from a silver bucket and peered inside. She used silver ice tongs to drop three cubes into a squat glass, then unstoppered an elegant cut-glass decanter and poured herself several fingers of amber liquid. "Haven't a clue," she said as she raised the glass to her lips. "He's a world traveler, remember? Why don't you try Madagascar for a start and move on from there?"

Before she could drink, the black glove seized her wrist and pulled it away from her mouth, slamming the heavy glass down onto the bar. Batman glared at her. "That's not what you told Arthur Reeves. You told him you were closer than ever to your father."

"Ah." Andrea's smile was unpleasant. "You've had me bugged, is that it?"

"I can read lips."

"Then read them now," she snarled. *"Get out."*

They held each other's stare for a tense moment. Then Batman turned and withdrew silently. He walked toward his reflection in the glass door, paused, and turned back to her. "Andrea. Why won't you tell me where your father is? Are you still following his orders?"

She had turned her back on him as he walked away. Now she looked disdainfully over her shoulder. "The way I see it," she drawled, "the only one in this room still controlled by his parents is you." She swirled the ice in her drink, then brought it to her lips, watching him coldly over the rim of the glass as she took a long swallow.

The Dark Knight stood motionless. Then his own

eyes grew cold and he vanished in a swirl of black cape through the balcony door.

Andrea took another drink. She waited almost a full minute, then walked slowly and deliberately over to the glass panel, swung it shut, and locked it tight. As she turned back to the bedroom, the glass slipped from her hand and fell to the floor. Ignoring the glass, Andrea walked stiffly to the bed and sat down. She raised her hands to cover her face as her shoulders shook gently. After a few moments, she curled her legs up onto the bed and began to weep quietly.

TWENTY-FOUR

The death's head mask seemed to float disembodied through the darkness, a trail of mist following it like a long gaseous cape. The apparition moved silently across the rooftops of Gotham City's lower east side. Then the black-clad figure paused as the town house of Sal Valestra came into view on the other side of the street.

Three minutes later, clouds of mist swirled around an upstairs window of the town house. The dark figure knelt on the windowsill and started to pry open the window as the smoky clouds grew and thickened. When the roiling mist cleared, the window was open and the narrow ledge outside it empty.

The eerie figure made its way cautiously through the halls of the old brownstone, drawn to its prey by the distant sound of wheezing laughter. The laughter grew gradually louder and more distinct as it slipped down the unlit passageway toward Valestra's den, until the dark mist curled directly outside a pair of sturdy

MASK OF THE PHANTASM

wooden doors. Black-gloved hands seized the ornate handles and pushed the doors wide.

The old mobster sat in his overstuffed chair in the center of the comfortable room. He was holding a page of Sunday comics close to his eyes, concealing his face. The wheezing laugh came again as the cloaked figure stepped soundlessly into the room.

Valestra continued to hold the paper close to his face as the apparition approached, taking no pains now to hide its presence. Standing before the easy chair, it pulled back its right arm and prepared to slash with the gleaming blade. *"Salvatore Valestra . . ."* it began in its droning voice. It reached in with its other hand and snatched away the paper.

Salvatore Valestra was wearing a dressing gown over his pants, with a small silken ascot at his neck in the style of years gone by. Rigged onto the mobster's sunken chest was a black box fitted with a miniature videocamera, a two-way radio, and a portable tape recorder. As the skull-headed figure stared down, the familiar wheezing laugh came again from the tape recorder. A green light shone steadily on the camera to indicate that it was transmitting.

Sal Valestra was dead, apparently of heart failure, his face contorted into an unrecognizable grin by the Joker's infamous nerve toxin. Shreds of newspaper remained wired to the dead man's bony hands.

The tiny camera swiveled with a whirring sound and pointed directly at the death's head mask.

"Whoops!" said a voice from the radio. "Guess the joke's on me—*you* don't seem to be the Dark Dimwit,

BATMAN: THE ANIMATED MOVIE

after all! Looks like we've got a new face in Gotham—if you call that a face.''

The apparition stepped back warily from the corpse, as a howl of maniacal laughter came from the radio. "Soon your name will be all over town," the voice continued, "to say nothing—"

The black-clad figure had been staring hard at the black box clasped against Valestra's unmoving chest. It turned suddenly and bolted through the door of the den, then dashed down the hallway toward the far window, mist curling frantically in its wake.

"—of your legs," the maniacal voice went on, "and your feet and your head and your spleen—"

The dark apparition dived out through the window just as the top floor of the town house erupted in a massive fireball.

TWENTY-FIVE

Detective Harvey Bullock
was sitting on the passenger side of a Gotham police
car, managing to gnaw on a cruller and slurp coffee
from a Styrofoam cup simultaneously, when the sky in
front of him was suddenly illuminated by a powerful
explosion. He lurched back in the seat, spilling coffee
and bits of doughnut on his stained overcoat as the
flash was followed by a reverberating boom.

Bullock turned to stare open-mouthed at the officer
behind the wheel. "Hey!" He smeared his hands on
the cracked upholstery. "I think that was old Sal Valestra's place!"

"Look there!" Renee Montoya pointed her brown
finger at the wavering outline of a dark, cloaked figure, barely visible as it ran behind a wall of concealing
mist atop a nearby building. The two stared at each
other for a beat. Then Montoya reached for the ignition, and the snub-nosed police car growled to life and

took off down the street, its lights flashing and its siren shrieking.

The Dark Knight was traversing Gotham in his own unique manner. He fired his grapple gun and swung between the tall buildings, his eyes on the city below. Fire and police sirens had begun to sound from several directions.

He made his way quickly to the section of the city known as Crime Alley. Finding a high vantage point, he scanned the rooftops in the vicinity of the blazing building. Almost immediately, he spied the black-garbed figure moving swiftly along the roof of an adjacent apartment complex. A pale headmask turned, as the other seemed to become aware of him at the same instant. Then a great cloud of mist boiled upward from the rooftop and the cloaked interloper took off in the opposite direction. The Dark Knight fired his grappling line and swung off in determined pursuit.

The death's head turned to peer back over its ragged shoulder several times as it glided away within its cloud of dark mist. There had been no sign of the Dark Knight since its first glimpse of him silhouetted against the high moon. Suddenly a dark shape swooped down out of nowhere, striking the black-clad apparition and knocking it to one side, out of the billowing mist.

The Dark Knight turned and faced his foe.

"This madness ends now," Batman said in a steely voice as his adversary rose silently to its feet. He aimed a crushing blow at the death's head mask. The dark wraith ducked, whirling swiftly to kick Batman squarely in the center of the bat emblem on his chest.

MASK OF THE PHANTASM

The Dark Knight gave a grunt of surprise and pain. Recovering quickly, he dropped down and spun around, thrusting out his boot to trip the other fighter. Then he grabbed his off-balance foe by the long ragged cloak and hauled the struggling figure up into the air. Just then the rhythmic sound of a helicopter's blades penetrated the noise of nearby traffic. The two dark figures turned to search the sky for the police copter.

The skull-masked figure activated its mist screen, at the same time delivering a sharp jab to Batman's jaw with its elbow. The Dark Knight's head snapped back. He stumbled backward a step and caught himself. Mist swirled up around his adversary as Batman rushed forward, groping through the thick clouds. In a rush of noise and wind, the police helicopter rose up behind him over the edge of the building. The clinging smoke dissipated sluggishly, revealing the Dark Knight alone on the rooftop.

"Batman! Stay where you are!" The officer's voice was amplified to a roar by his bullhorn. His words boomed out over the sound of the rotors, as a brilliant spotlight beam snapped on beneath the copter, washing the rooftop in cold white light. The Dark Knight hesitated for a fraction of a second, then turned to dash into the shadows.

"Stay on him," the officer ordered his pilot. The helicopter dipped below the structure and accelerated to the left, skimming above the lower rooftops in pursuit of the fleeing Batman. The Dark Knight made his way skillfully from one building to the next, jumping, dodging, and employing his grapple line as the copter strove to keep up with him.

"He's been warned." The officer in the helicopter drew his gun. "We were told to treat him as armed and extremely dangerous." He bit his lower lip, then aimed carefully at the dodging figure and pulled the trigger. Batman dived off the edge of a ramshackle factory as the first round of bullets whizzed past his cowl and shattered several windows.

He fell five yards, landing heavily on the ledge of a lower building. He took a moment to catch his breath. The spotlight caught him as he rolled to his feet. He sprang from the ledge to land catlike on the flattened head of a massive, birdlike gargoyle. A row of six of the stone monsters protruded from the side of a building which housed law offices. Batman began to leap from head to head, shots ringing in his ears as the helicopter followed in close pursuit.

He fired his grapple gun and dived from the last gargoyle, his line bringing him swinging past the window of a ninth floor apartment. Inside, a middle-aged woman named Sophia was just settling down in her bath with a copy of the latest true romance novel. As the black figure swooped past her bathroom window she shrieked and ducked under the water, paperback and all.

The Dark Knight somersaulted onto a fire escape ladder. The rusty contraption unfolded with a protracted screeching sound, lowering slowly under his weight until its end hung ten feet above a cluttered alley. Clotheslines crowded with socks and underwear crisscrossed the upper levels of the alley. The helicopter hovered indecisively between the two buildings, then gave up and veered back up into the sky.

Batman released his hold on the fire escape and dropped into the refuse beneath him. His left leg caught on a discarded tricycle and twisted painfully. He straightened slowly and started to limp toward the end of the alley.

"Freeze!" yelled Harvey Bullock. Batman wheeled around to find himself staring into the barrels of a dozen guns.

He pointed his grapple gun upward and fired. He activated the reeling mechanism on the side of the gun, swinging up and away just as the officers charged forward. He soared on the line up over the creased forehead of a grinning stone demon leaning out from a lower level of the legal building. He kicked against the broad brow and leaped off into space, twisting his body to send him plunging through the open walls of the half-completed structure of a new apartment complex. He landed awkwardly on a wooden platform suspended within the skeletal structure.

He moved around warily on the flimsy platform, as flashlight beams played among the upright struts. Then a loud report came from below, and a small metal cylinder lobbed into view. The canister landed on the wooden platform a yard from the Dark Knight's boots, detonating on impact. It was tear gas. Batman staggered back, coughing hoarsely as he fumbled at his utility belt.

Down the street a huge police SWAT van had rolled up. The massive vehicle disgorged its passengers, the officers fanning out around the incomplete building.

BATMAN: THE ANIMATED MOVIE

As he sank to his knees in the shadow of a dumpster, one of the SWAT team officers cupped his ear and looked up. "I hear him!" the man called. "He's right there—" He squinted up into the dark building and squeezed off a round of machine-gun fire.

"Wait!" Harvey Bullock bellowed from the mouth of the alley. The burly detective charged toward the man. "No one fires till I give the word!"

Up above, Batman pulled a compacted gas mask from his belt as the volley of gunfire from the street splintered the half-finished ceiling above his head. It hung creaking as the dust settled, and he thought it was going to hold. But the floor above was loaded with tool boxes and heavy machinery, and it suddenly gave way, collapsing on the Dark Knight, its weight sending him crashing in turn through the overburdened floor on which he stood. He landed twelve feet below amid a shower of debris. His teeth closed on his lower lip as his back struck something solid.

"Get a light up there!" Bullock ordered. He squinted up into the darkness. Tear gas still billowed from one of the unfinished floors. A minute later a spotlight shot its wide beam upward and began to play over the skeletal building.

As the beam swept slowly through the struts and girders, Batman began to push his way laboriously out of the wreckage. His back felt as if it had been struck repeatedly by a sledgehammer. His cowl had been torn open by the fall and he was bleeding from several cuts to the face and body. He touched his hand to the back of his head and stared at the patch of slick blood on his glove. In the distance the sound of the helicopter blades returned.

Batman groaned in pain. His vision was getting blurry. He could dimly see the helicopter hanging like a great dark dragonfly outside the building. He drew the grapple gun painfully from his belt.

"I think I see some movement," the officer in the helicopter told the pilot. "Circle back there." His eyes grew wide in amazement as a metal grapple hit the copter's landing skid and attached itself with a dull *clang*. "Hey!"

The pilot leaned out of his open door, staring downward in shock. "I can't believe it," he said. "He's climbing on. He's coming to get us!" The copter rocked as he snatched the other officer's gun from his hand and began to fire erratically at the dangling figure.

On the ground, the leader of the SWAT team pulled her own gun and pointed to the dark figure that swung wildly below the bucking helicopter. "There he is! Fire!"

A hail of bullets from several directions ripped into the cloaked figure, which bounced and jerked spasmodically at the multiple impact. The cape was gradually being ripped to shreds. Finally it dropped away, revealing a bullet-riddled sawhorse securely attached to the grapple line beneath the copter. The SWAT leader's mouth fell open. "Quick!" she shouted. "Around the back!"

With neither his cape nor his cowl, dressed in the bloody tatters of his uniform, Bruce Wayne slid down a construction cable toward the street on the far side of the building. The back of his head was sticky with blood. He dropped the last few inches, his knees buckling on impact. Then he staggered back to his feet. He looked around as he heard the police approaching.

"This way!" someone cried.

Bruce shook his head dazedly, trying to clear his vision as a mob of distant, blurry shapes surged around the corner of the building. "You! Stop!" came the growling voice of Detective Bullock.

Bruce clenched his jaw and lurched forward, concentrating on each successive moment. He bolted across the street and loped down an alley. At the end of the alley was a low fence, which he struggled over, his movements stiff and awkward. Then he was on another street, beginning to run again as lights brightened behind him. He looked back over his shoulder and saw a police car gaining steadily on him with the inexorability of a nightmare. He spotted a black crevice between two buildings and ducked suddenly to the right, limping down the tight alleyway as the squad car screeched to a halt. Officers poured into the alley after him, stumbling and cursing as they picked their way through mounds of rubble.

Bruce reached the far end of the alley just as a small, two-seater convertible shot into view. The car skidded to a stop, blocking his exit. He was turning back into the alley when the door on the passenger side swung open and a slender figure leaned out, gesturing for him to get in.

Bruce shook his head groggily. "Andrea . . . ?" he said. It was getting difficult to make sense of things.

"Hurry!"

Bullock's officers were nearing the end of the alley. He could hear their shouts as he swayed on the filthy sidewalk.

Summoning up his last reserve of strength, he vaulted forward and tumbled into the car. Andrea floored the gas pedal and the tiny vehicle streaked away.

TWENTY-SIX

Burton Earny was heading home after his first long day of odd jobs at the Park Row Community Center when he realized that he'd forgotten his camera. He stopped in the middle of the sidewalk and squinched his eyes shut, trying to remember the last place he'd put it down.

There. He opened his eyes. He had brought it with him into Dr. Thompkins's office when he'd first gone in to straighten up her files. A banana and a small package of peanut butter–filled rye crackers—today's snack and lunch respectively—had been in the rumpled paper bag along with the camera, and Burt had planned to eat while he worked. As it turned out, he had become too absorbed in the filing system he was creating to think about food—a first for Burton—and then the people at the center had surprised him by asking him to join them in the outer room for the modest hot lunch they provided for the neighborhood.

This neighborhood could use all the help it could

get, Burt mused, turning around in his tracks and starting to trudge back down Finger Avenue in the direction of the center. While they ate their lunch, Maggie
Price, the large, dark-skinned woman who had been
Burt's supervisor for most of the day, had filled him
in on the decline and eventual fall of the once-fashionable area known as Park Row.

Burt shivered in the evening coolness, pulling the
collar of his jacket up under his round chin. Now they
called it Crime Alley, and according to Maggie Price
it was not the kind of place that would ever appear on
the "Sightseeing Maps of Old Gotham" Burt had seen
for sale in the bus depot. The way Maggie told it,
worsening economic conditions, combined with the
gradual infestation of certain mob elements, had dealt
Park Row a blow that it had been trying to recover
from for over thirty years. And—according to Maggie
and just about everyone else Burt had spoken to over
the course of the long day—it was a blow that would
have been fatal, were it not for the almost single-
handed intervention of one very special person.

Dr. Leslie Thompkins had been born in this neighborhood back when it was the abode of the successful
and the well-to-do rather than the rats and the mug-
gers. She had come of age amid the wealth of Park
Row, had attended parties here with the other social-
ites of her circle, and returned from medical school to
open up a small but lucrative practice not far from the
converted storefront where the Community Center
now stood.

Unlike most of her peers, Leslie Thompkins had re-
sisted the urge to flee to higher ground when the tides

of change threatened to sink Park Row. Dr. T.—as the habitués of the Community Center lovingly called her—had not only stood her ground, she had actually made that ground flourish, making up in lives saved and friendships won what she had lost in prestige and income. Now, when sickness threatened the neighborhood children or poverty ravaged its elderly, Dr. T. was there with free medical care, a decent meal, or just a friendly ear. And when bulldozers had threatened the Community Center itself, she had marched down to City Hall with a homemade placard and testified before the Zoning Board with her friends, a straight-backed defender of the rights of the poor and disadvantaged.

Burton quickened his step a little. Shadows were lengthening in the doorways and alleys, and he didn't like the idea of having to make his way back through these streets after it had become truly dark. For one thing, the streetlights that actually functioned seemed to be limited to one per block; and for another, Burt's sense of direction was so poor that he could conceivably wander the same block for hours without finding his way back to the subway station.

He had gotten the job at the Community Center by being lost, in fact, reading about it on the small square of paper he had found tacked to a utility pole not far from here. He had been heading for a job interview in an entirely different section of the city, when one misstep had led to another and he had found himself hopelessly adrift in this rundown neighborhood.

For the first time that he could remember, getting lost had had its benefits. The odd jobs that needed doing at the center had held his attention for the long hours that he worked on them and were certainly more satisfying, if not more financially rewarding, than the position sorting colored chalk that he had been planning to interview for. Mrs. Price had taken him under her wing immediately, providing him with a tour of the center as she outlined the many tasks that absolutely needed to be done if they were to keep things in good running order. For hours, Burt had organized filing cabinets, scraped and painted walls, read to a group of preschoolers whose parents could not afford day care, and carried donated meals to a small group of locals who were too ill to leave their apartments. One of them, a man of about Burt's own age who had been so thin and wasted that he could barely sit up on the edge of the bed to eat his lunch, had practically wept in gratitude for the kindness of his neighbors. Burt had transferred a small apple from his paper bag to his jacket pocket before he left the center, in case he found himself in need of a pick-me-up while he made his rounds. After the thin man had mentioned a fondness for fresh fruit, Burt had quietly slipped the apple out of his pocket and sliced it up for the two of them, making sure the other man got most of the slices.

Burt had fetched and carried, scraped and filed, till Maggie Price had had to come into Dr. Thompkins's empty office at half past six and take him by the elbow, forcibly showing him the cracked face of the old clock in the outer room and telling him it was time to stop. Even then she had practically had to throw him out the door, for he had noticed several things on his way out of the office that could have stood fixing right at that moment. That was when he had forgotten his camera, he realized. He had been so focused on the many tasks at hand that he hadn't given a thought to the one material possession that meant more to him than any other.

He was making his way down the last block, the yellow light of the center doorway blazing cheerfully ahead of him, when he saw the terrific flash in the sky to the east, like a giant flashbulb going off above the tops of nearby buildings. Then came the explosion, a sound sharper than thunder, that shook him up through the soles of his feet and made the tenement windows rattle in their frames. Burt stood stock-still, his mouth gaping wide, as doors creaked open and people poured out into the street. He took off down the block at a jog, threading his way among chattering children and bleary-eyed derelicts as he joined the general migration toward the center.

Maggie Price was standing at the top of the steps when he puffed up, a formidable scowl on her broad brown face, and her hands planted firmly on her wide hips.

"I—forgot—something—" Burt huffed. "What was—that?"

Maggie's eyes were narrowed to slits. "I don't know, but I can tell you who's most likely behind it. I knew we hadn't heard the last from that ol' weasel, *Daggett*!" She spat the name out as if it left a bad taste in her mouth.

"It wasn't Daggett this time." Another woman had come hurrying up the street, pulling a thin young girl wearing an odd black hood over her head. "Sam Weed says it was one a' them brownstones over on Shays Street. He thinks it's where that skinny old gentleman who used to walk around with the oxygen bottle lived. No reason for Roland Daggett to try his 'urban renewal' in that partic'lar neighborhood."

"No, but he might a' done it for a different reason." A short, stocky man with a huge scar on the top of his bald head spoke up in the gathering crowd. "That old guy's Sal Valestra. Used ta be a mob boss 'fore he retired from it."

"Hmmmph." Mrs. Price shook her head disapprovingly. "Like you can retire from the mob like it was a job at the bank."

"Way some a' dem haul in d' cash, das jus' what it is!" cackled a tiny old woman with gray braids wrapped around her narrow skull. "A job at d' bank!" The crowd laughed.

"Well, perhaps we'd better all come inside and see what we can find out."

The clear voice belonged to someone Burt hadn't seen before. She had come out of the center to stand beside Maggie. She was a thin, handsome woman in her mid-sixties, with a compassionate face Burt found himself instantly drawn to. The people gathered outside the steps responded to her suggestion at once, filing in past her with nods and murmured words of greeting.

"Dr. T., I want you to meet somebody." Maggie took Burt's arm and pulled him to the side of the doorway as the others went past. "This is Mr. Earny, Burt Earny, and he's been helpin' us out all day. He saw that ad we put up about odd jobs and came right over." She gave Burt an admiring glance. "He's just about done 'em all today, too—an' told me he's ready to come back tomorrow."

"I'm certainly glad to meet you, Burt." The doctor held out a thin hand and Burt shook it shyly. "I was just admiring some of your handiwork in my office. You have a real knack for organization." She turned to Maggie with a smile. "I should get out of here more often!"

"It was fun," Burt told her, realizing as he said the words that they were true. "I do want to come back tomorrow."

"Well, that's fine." Dr. Thompkins smiled warmly. "You're certainly needed here, though we can't afford to pay you very much. And now—" She raised her eyes to the glow of orange that flickered beyond the rooftops. "We'd better get on the phone and see if there's anybody over there in need of help. Oh—" She paused, turning to reach for something sitting behind her on a small table. "This wouldn't be yours, by any chance, would it?" She held out Burt's paper bag.

"Yes, thanks. My camera." Burt took the sack from her. "And a banana."

"And a small package of peanut butter crackers. I checked." Dr. Thompkins smiled again and disappeared into her cramped office.

"Wanna get some big cash money?" The tiny woman with the braids had stepped up to stand at Burt's elbow. "Jus' take d' camera over to d' fire 'n' git a pitcha dat ol' man all toasted up like a marshy-mellow. Papers give ya hunnerd bucks, y' gotta pitcha like dat!''

Maggie Price laid her large arm on the old woman's bowed shoulders. ''Miss Rosey here's what you might call our financial expert,'' she told Burt with a wink. ''Still, if you do have a camera in there, she's probably right. You run over and get a couple good shots of the firemen, it might be worth it.''

Burt shook his head. ''I'd probably be more useful staying here, in case there's somebody that needs help. Anyway, I already tried taking a picture of a disaster the other day.'' He gave the two women a brief rundown of his experience at the Grand Imperator. ''I was there for a job interview,'' he concluded. ''But I didn't get it.'' He looked around the room, now bustling with activity as the volunteers checked on food and medical supplies while they awaited word of the explosion. ''Now I'm kinda glad they turned me down.''

''I heard all 'bout dat car got stuck in d' wall,'' Miss Rosey piped up. ''Say d' back door open up and money jus' pour outta dat car like salt fum a shaker!'' She cackled with glee at the notion.

''You think you got some good pictures of it?'' Maggie asked him. ''Maybe you can still sell 'em.''

Burt was doubtful. ''Well, I know I messed up the first one, on account of not being ready for it to happen. Then I took six or seven of the car from different angles. I don't know how they came out.'' He pulled the shiny black camera out of the bag. ''I didn't want to try and get it developed till I shot the rest of the roll, though. It's pretty expensive film.'' He looked around the bustling room again, noting the smiles and the friendly faces. "I think I have an idea how I want to use it up now, though," he said. He lifted the camera and slipped the strap over his neck.

"Dat a yella banana I see in dat sack?" Miss Rosey was peering down the wrinkled neck of Burt's paper bag, the tip of her tongue resting on her lower lip as she craned up on tiptoe. "Bin a *long* time I tasted a real banana."

"Sure." Burt slid the fruit from the bag and passed it to the old woman. "I've got some rye crackers, too, if you want 'em. Only stand over there, where I can get a good shot of you with the other volunteers. You too, Mrs. Price."

"Don't know why you'd want a picture of this rag-tag lot," said the large woman, steering Miss Rosey over to a group that was counting blankets. "And it's Maggie, young man."

"Okay, Maggie." Burt grinned. "Now say 'cheese.' "

"Dis a b'nana," Miss Rosey muttered around a mouthful of mushy fruit. "Any fool see dat."

The last picture Burt took was of the little girl with the homemade black hood. She posed on the back of an old couch in the middle of the big room, her fists on her hips and her thin chest stuck out proudly.

"Name's Tansy," said the girl's mother as Burt's camera rewound the film with a soft whirr. "Though lately she answers mostly to Batwoman, hero of Park Row."

Burt nodded, blinking dubiously. "They're saying Batman's the one who killed those two gangsters," he

MASK OF THE PHANTASM

said. "The man in the sports car I took pictures of and that other one out at the cemetery." He shivered.

"They know what's good for 'em, they better not be sayin' that 'round here," the girl's mother told him. "Dr. Thompkins got a soft spot for the Batman. She says it's all a frame-up." She fastened a brightly printed scarf around her springy hair and called out to her daughter. "You want to collect your doll, little Batwoman? Time we were headin' home."

Tansy leaped down to the cracked linoleum and paused to adjust her black construction paper mask. "Robin!" she called, bending to search under the sofa.

Her mother turned back to Burt. "What Dr. T. says, is folks oughtta have a little faith in somebody who's tried his best to help 'em." She held out her hand to her daughter, who was cradling a Raggedy Andy dressed in red and green felt in her thin brown arms. "And *I* say Dr. T. is a very smart lady."

The repercussions of the firebombing of Salvatore Valestra's brownstone gradually came to light as the evening wore on in Crime Alley. Following the initial explosion, flames had leaped to a long-abandoned buggy whip factory on the other side of the street and from there to two nearby rooftops, demolishing both tenements, one long deserted and the other newly occupied, before the fire fighters were able to get the blaze under control.

By the time Burt finally left the center, he and the others had provided food and shelter to nine families left homeless by the fire. It was past ten o'clock when

he walked down the front steps. He was exhausted—
and more satisfied than he could remember feeling in
years.

Maggie Price walked him to the end of the street.
"You did a good week's worth a' work here today,
Burt," she told him as they stood on the pavement
outside her small apartment. "If you're not too tired
out, we'd sure be glad to see your face around here
again tomorow."

"I'll be here," he said. "I want to drop off my film
at the Kwik-shot, and then I'll come right on down."
He paused. "I saw Dr. Thompkins on the phone on
my way out. She didn't look too good. Is something
wrong?"

Maggie heaved her shoulders in a shrug. "Radio's
been sayin' Batman was seen outside of that place that
burned. You know that old man was a gangster, just
like the other two. Police went after Batman with hel-
icopters and SWAT cops and what all else they had,
accordin' to the news. Didn't catch him, but they
think they roughed him up pretty bad." She shook her
head. "Might surprise some folks to know it, but Dr.
T. thinks quite highly of the Batman. She won't sleep
tonight till she finds out he's all right. . . ."

TWENTY-SEVEN

"There are certain advantages to having a sturdy cranium, Master Bruce."

Alfred wrapped the last of several layers of bandages around his employer's head and stepped back to inspect his handiwork. Bruce was sitting shirtless on the edge of his bed, his lower body still clad in Batman's gray tights and black boots. Small bandages dotted his torso, and bruises were beginning to appear like isolated storm clouds. Andrea Beaumont sat next to him on the bed.

"But then," the butler finished with an ironic smile, "hardheadedness has always been your cardinal virtue." He began gathering up his medical supplies, piling them on a silver tray that sat on the bureau. "I have received several telephone calls from Dr. Thompkins this evening, inquiring about your whereabouts and physical condition. With your permission, I will inform her of your relative well-being, now that I am assured of it myself."

"Yes, thank you, Alfred."

The butler's eyes widened a fraction as Andrea laid her hand on Bruce's arm. "Well." He gave a small cough. "I'm sure I must have things to do elsewhere. . . ." He exited the room discreetly.

Bruce lifted Andrea's hand from his arm and held it in both of his. "You have an excellent sense of timing," he said softly.

"It was all on TV," Andrea replied. "I had to do something. Good thing my hotel wasn't too far away . . ."

Bruce raised his hand to her face, touching her cheek with his fingertips. Andrea shivered, turning away slightly under his touch.

Bruce took a breath. "I'm grateful, of course," he said, withdrawing his hand. He exhaled. "But I still need to know why you're not telling me the truth about your father."

Andrea hesitated, her blue-green eyes probing Bruce's face. Then she gave a dispirited shrug and reached for her purse. She removed the photo Batman had given her earlier that evening and held it in both hands in her lap. "Well," she said with a sigh, "I suppose the world's greatest detective would find out eventually, one way or the other. You remember that evening when you . . ." She swallowed, started again, a faraway look coming into her eyes as she peered back through the years. "You remember Daddy was having a meeting with his 'partners' that night. . . ."

Andrea had kept her eyes focused carefully in front of her as she passed Valestra's tall driver on her way into the house, ignoring both the throaty growl and the wide leer. She closed the front door softly behind her and paused in the foyer. Muted voices came from beyond the open door of her father's study. They grew louder as she headed down the short corridor.

"It ain't right, Carl," Chuckie Sol was saying in cajoling tones. "You're a businessman—you know that."

"Yeah," seconded the deeper voice of Buzz Bronski. "You've taken what's ours, Beaumont. Now you're gonna pay for it—one way or another."

Alarmed, Andrea hurried the last few steps and burst into the study. Her father sat on the far side of his desk, the three gangsters leaning over him. On his haggard face was the expression of a trapped animal.

"What are you doing?" Andrea cried. "Leave him alone!"

"Well, well." Sal Valestra turned his head slowly and regarded Andrea through a thick cloud of cigar smoke. "The little girl's home. I'm sorry you had to see this, Ms. Beaumont."

Andrea took a step back under the sinister gaze. Buzz Bronski moved quickly behind her and grabbed her arm, twisting it up against her back.

Andrea used a quick judo move to break the hold, then slashed out at Bronski with the side of her hand. Luck, rather than skill, allowed the burly mobster to block her blow. He reached out a muscular arm and twisted her around, locking his thick forearm around her neck. Andrea gasped in pain as he tightened his grip.

"Stop it! Let her go!" Beaumont rose up from his

chair in horror. He stumbled out from behind the desk and lunged toward Bronski, his own arm raised.

"Watch it, Pops." Chuckie Sol was on him from behind, grabbing him by the elbows and dragging him back.

"Yeah, Pops." Bronski grinned at the stricken Beaumont, his arm squeezing tighter around the base of Andrea's throat. She clawed at him futilely, struggling to breathe.

Beaumont's demeanor changed instantly. "Please, Sal." He turned back to Valestra. "Don't let him hurt her. I'm begging you!" He dropped to his knees on the carpet, his face twisted with anguish. "Give me another day—one more day! I swear I'll get the money!"

Valestra looked from the businessman to his daughter. He raised his index finger to Bronski and the heavy gangster eased up slightly on the girl's throat. "Convince me, Carl," Valestra said softly.

"On—on my mother's grave," Beaumont pleaded. "Tomorrow. This time tomorrow. I *swear*!"

Andrea watched her father incredulously.

"As soon as the European banks open," Beaumont went on, "I'll make the transaction and have the whole amount wired to you."

Valestra watched Beaumont grovel with an amused expression. He glanced up at Chuckie Sol and raised a thin gray eyebrow. Sol pursued his lips and nodded. Valestra turned to Bronski. "Okay," said the heavy mobster, his arm still pressed against Andrea's throat.

Valestra drew on his cigar, its tip flaring bright orange as he considered the request. He glanced down at the kneeling Beaumont and released a large puff of smoke directly into the other man's face. "Lucky for you my partners and I are compassionate men." He leaned down, pointing a bony finger at Carl Beaumont's face. "Twenty-four hours. This time tomorrow, we'll have our money—or *I'll* have your heart in my hand." He closed his fingers into a fist and withdrew it slowly as he straightened. He took another draw on the cigar and nodded toward the doorway. "Let's go, boys."

Bronski unfolded his arm and propelled Andrea toward her father with a shove in the small of her back. Andrea stood stunned in the middle of the floor, breathing in deep gasps.

Chuckie Sol gave her an evil grin as he sidled past. As Valestra headed for the doorway, he pointed his index finger at the two Beaumonts and cocked his thumb as if it were the hammer of a revolver, making a small clicking noise with his tongue. He joined his cohorts at the door and the three men began a low-voiced discussion as they strolled out of the room, Bronski glancing back over his shoulder to smile a last smug smile at Andrea.

She waited till she heard the front door close, then rushed to her father's side. He was still kneeling on the carpet where Valestra had left him. "Dad—are you all right? Should I get the police?"

Beaumont brushed her hands away and got shakily to his feet. He was staring at the doorway. "Pack a suitcase," he said to Andrea. "Now! We've got to get to the airport."

"What . . . ?" She stared at him in disbelief as he

BATMAN: THE ANIMATED MOVIE

started to shove papers from the top of his desk into his briefcase. "But you said you'd have their money—"

"It's not that simple." He moved to a pair of oak file cabinets and began opening and closing the drawers. "The money's all tied up in investments. Could take weeks to free it up."

"But—but I can't leave!" Andrea stood dumbfounded in the center of the room. She had never seen her father behave like this before. She strode to his side and slammed the file drawer shut, forcing him to look at her. "Dad, Bruce proposed to me tonight— we're going to get married!"

"Listen to me!" Beaumont grabbed his daughter by the shoulders. His thumbs dug into her flesh. "I just used up the last shred of so-called compassion that Salvatore Valestra possesses. If I don't pay him back within twenty-four hours, they will hunt us down and they will most certainly kill us both!" He gave her shoulders a shake on the word "kill." He steered her to the window and pried the blinds open a fraction. "Look!"

Andrea leaned forward to peer through the narrow crack. There was a single car left in the driveway. She could make out the tall driver reclining with a magazine in the front seat.

"You see?" Beaumont hissed. "One way or another, they'll get what they want."

Andrea pulled back from the window. Tears began to well in her eyes as she studied her father's panicked face. "How—why did you do this, Dad? Why did you get involved with those people . . . ?"

"I'm sorry, Andi." Beaumont took her hand and pressed it to his cheek. "I—I just wanted a chance for you—I—" He pulled back an inch and drew himself up. "I'll get us out of this," he swore. "Somehow we'll be free of them—no matter what it takes. That's a promise."

Fifteen minutes later, the tall man was sitting in the car playing solitaire when two shadowy figures darted furtively from the rear of the house and into the woods beyond. Each carried a suitcase.

The night wind whistled through the car window and the tall man looked up from shuffling the deck. Was that a noise? A gray squirrel leaped from a nearby telephone line and landed awkwardly on a thin branch overhanging the car. The tall man reached stealthily for the revolver lying next to him on the front seat. "C'mon, Rocky," he coaxed, pulling back the hammer. Chittering with excitement, the squirrel regained its balance and scampered up the branch into the foliage. The tall man replaced the gun on the seat with a shrug and returned to his card game.

"We hid all over Europe."

Andrea stared at the floor, her hand knotting the bedspread at her side as she finished her story. "Eventually we settled on the Mediterranean coast. Dad was able to parlay the money he'd embezzled into a small fortune. Finally he had enough to pay them back—or so he thought." She raised her eyes to Bruce. They had a haunted look. "But when he contacted them, it turned out it wasn't enough. It would *never* be enough. They wanted interest and they wanted it compounded in blood." She lowered her gaze again. "He had to find another way."

Bruce nodded grimly. "The man in the costume I saw tonight—your father?"

Andrea rubbed her fingertips across her forehead. "He said we'd be free of them somehow. When I heard about Chuckie Sol . . . I had to come back. To find him." She bit her lower lip. "To stop him."

She picked up her purse and rose from the bed, looking down at Bruce with a lost expression. "I'm sorry, Bruce. That's twice now I've come into your life and messed it up."

Bruce got to his feet with a wince of pain as she started for the door. His legs were still wobbly when he crossed the room and took her into his arms. He wiped the tears from her cheek with his fingers.

He was still holding her when Alfred entered with a tea tray a minute later. The butler turned smoothly on his heel and left the room. Neither Bruce nor Andrea noticed.

The phone was ringing by the time Alfred reached the kitchen. He set the tray down on a counter and lifted the receiver. "Wayne Manor."

"How is he, Alfred?" The youthful voice at the other end of the line was tinged with urgency. "Is he okay?"

"Quite well, Master Dick, aside from the customary near-mortal injuries routinely suffered by persons with your, shall we say, less than prudent avocation."

There was a pause. "You did say he was all right somewhere back at the beginning there, didn't you?"

The butler allowed himself a tiny smile. "I did indeed, Master Dick. The wounds have been cleaned and the bandages are in place. No need to be over-concerned about Master Bruce's physical condition."

"That's a relief. I'm in the middle of exams, but the TV made it sound pretty grim, and I could be outta here like a shot if you guys need me. Hey, wait a minute—what did you mean about his 'physical' condition? Is there something going on with Bruce's head?"

"Nothing for which a cure currently exists, I'm afraid," Alfred replied.

"Why are you being so mysterious about this, Alfred? Is Bruce okay or not? Can I talk to him?"

"I would advise against it at the moment," Alfred said. "The young lady and he seem to have some 'catching up to do,' as the phrase goes."

"Young lady? Oh, I get it. . . . Which one is it this time, Alfred? Or do we even know her name yet?"

"We most assuredly do, Master Dick." The butler's expression sobered. "The young lady's name is Andrea Beaumont."

"Andrea—" The young man gave a low whistle as puzzlement turned to revelation. "Wow, that was before I even knew Bruce. What's she doing back in town? And how is Bruce taking it?"

"I cannot say what Miss Beaumont's purpose is in returning to Gotham City," Alfred said. "And as for your second question . . ."

BATMAN: THE ANIMATED MOVIE

"Yeah, I shouldn't have bothered to ask. When have we ever known what was really going on inside him?"

Alfred nodded into the receiver. "Precisely, Master Dick."

TWENTY-EIGHT

The following morning Bruce stood in his light blue pajama bottoms in the doorway that opened from his bedroom onto the patio. It seemed to him that the sun was shining more brightly this morning than he had ever seen it before. Andrea was on the patio, pouring herself a cup of coffee from a small tray heaped with muffins and croissants. She was wearing the top to a pair of blue pajamas. The breeze played with her hair.

Bruce crossed the patio and put his arms around her from behind, drawing her close. Andrea closed her eyes and leaned back against his chest, smiling. She placed the cup back on the tray and turned to face him.

"Can we make it work this time, Bruce?" She reached her arms up and laced her fingers behind his neck.

"I want to say yes." His expression was tentative. "But you know it's going to come down to me against your father."

Andrea rested her head on Bruce's chest and stared out over the rolling landscape. Far in the distance, blue-green water sparkled in the sunlight. "Daddy doesn't matter anymore," she said softly.

It was noon before she left the mansion. She had put the top down on her convertible. When Bruce leaned over to give her a kiss, Andrea's elbow bumped the steering wheel and the horn gave a sharp bleat. They leaped apart at the noise, then laughed.

"I'll see you tonight," she told him.

"I'll be here."

She drove off with a wave. Alfred stepped out of the main doors, his prim features almost cheerful. "It's good to see you and Miss Beaumont together again, sir," he commented as they watched the small car disappear onto the road at the end of the driveway. Bruce turned to go inside. As he was mounting the steps toward the house, Alfred asked, "Might one inquire what this portends for your alter ego?"

Bruce's step slowed. His shoulders slumped as if a heavy burden had just been returned to them. "I'm not sure, Alfred. So much has changed."

He entered his study and walked to the broad mahogany desk. Photos littered the desk top. The black-and-white picture of Carl Beaumont seated in the restaurant with the three gangsters stood out among laughing snapshots of Bruce and Andrea taken in happier times.

Three *dead* gangsters, Bruce thought as he lifted the photo from the pile and studied it.

"You still love each other." Alfred had followed

MASK OF THE PHANTASM

him into the room. "That much, as least, has not changed."

"It's true," Bruce said. "I do love her. Maybe . . . after all this is settled . . ." He set down the picture and raised his eyes to the wall where the portrait of his parents hung. "Maybe then . . ."

"I'm certain they would have wanted you to be happy, Master Bruce," Alfred said, following the younger man's gaze. With the light of a bright day streaming in through the window, the portrait seemed less austere and forbidding. As Bruce examined his parents' faces, the expressions that had seemed disapproving looked more like melancholy smiles. He gave a small shrug, dropping his gaze to the desk top. He frowned and picked up the photograph of the gangsters again.

Alfred looked down past the younger man's shoulder at the photo. "Is something wrong?"

Bruce narrowed his eyes at the picture. His gaze scanned the four familiar faces, then lingered for the first time on the fifth member of Beaumont's group, the tall, gaunt man who lurked mostly in shadow behind the businessman's back. Bruce rubbed his chin thoughtfully. There was something. . . .

Alfred blinked in surprise as Bruce reached past him to pluck a red pencil from a cup at the edge of the desk. He lowered the pencil point to the photo and touched it tentatively to the portion of the tall man's face that was clearly lit. Starting on the left cheek, he made a shallow arc beneath the long nose, a thin red line that ran from one side of the face to the other. Returning to his starting point, he drew another,

BATMAN: THE ANIMATED MOVIE

deeper curve, below the first one. His eyes widened with a look of dread.

"Oh no," he whispered, holding the photo up to the cheery light from the window. The long jaw of Valestra's driver was now split sideways by a leering maniacal grin. A peal of shrieking laughter began somewhere in the back of Bruce's mind as he stared at the distorted visage. He gave his head a savage shake, his expression growing fierce.

"No," he said again.

TWENTY-NINE

Storm clouds were gathering in the late afternoon sky above Gotham City. Councilman Arthur Reeves scowled out the window of his spacious office on the tenth floor of City Hall, his mood matching the approaching turbulence.

"You're telling me there were four precincts on Batman's heels and he *still* got away?" Reeves shouted into the phone. He was pacing rapidly back and forth as he spoke. A thin line of lightning lit the darkening sky some distance away.

"Unbelievable! Incredible!" Reeves slammed the receiver down into its cradle and glared at it.

Thunder rumbled outside the building.

"*Tsk! Tsk!* And to think our hard-earned tax money goes to pay those slackers in blue!"

Reeves spun around in shock at the sound of the voice. His blood chilled at the sight that greeted him. "You!"

"*Moi,*" his visitor admitted with a small bow. The

BATMAN: THE ANIMATED MOVIE

Joker was dressed in a purple topcoat, with a wide-brimmed purple hat set at a rakish angle above his white face. He stood in the office doorway and tapped his long, thin cane on the carpeted floor.

Reeves's face had drained of blood till it almost matched his visitor's pallor. He turned on his heel and raced for the other door.

The Joker stifled a yawn. "That's right, little Artie, run for help." He leaned back against the doorframe with a smug laugh. "Call the cops. Call the marines. Bring in the gentlemen and ladies of the press, why don't cha?" He lifted his hands to frame his face, mugging for imaginary photographers. "Quite a photo op: the esteemed councilman and his oh-so-wacky pal."

Reeves hesitated at the other door, his hand on the burnished knob. "You're no friend of mine," he said sullenly.

"What?" The Joker's grin twisted into an exaggerated grimace of pain. "Artie, I'm crushed!" The clown clutched at his mustard-colored vest. "How quickly the high and mighty forget the little folk!" The tall figure left the doorway and sauntered over to Reeves's desk. He seated himself in the comfortable chair and propped his long legs on the desk top. "Don't cha remember the good ol' days, Artie—you, me, Sallie, and the gang?"

The councilman released the doorknob and moved back toward the desk. "I never met them or you," he declared in a self-righteous tone. Anger was beginning to outweigh the fear in his mind at the thought of any connection between himself and this murderous buffoon. "I worked for Carl Beaumont—period. I didn't know what he was doing, or who he did it for."

"Oh, maybe not at the beginning." The clown swiveled in the chair and reached for a gleaming silver letter opener, in the shape of a tiny sword. He began to mime cleaning beneath his gloved fingernails. "But you knew about it afterwards, all right." He tilted the brim of his hat back with the letter opener and flashed Reeves a conspiratorial grin. "And put it to darn good use, eh what?"

Shock and fear returned momentarily to Reeves's handsome face. His jaw pushed angrily forward as he regained control of himself. "What do you want?" he asked coldly.

The Joker examined the letter opener in his palm for a casual moment. Then he reared back and stabbed the silver sword into the desk top, rage blazing in his black-ringed eyes. "To find out who's iced the old gang!" he said in a venomous voice. The mobile face became a distorted tragedy mask as he rose from the chair and leaned on the desk. "Charlton, Joseph, Salvatore—all my little playmates gone . . ." He wiped an imaginary tear from his bleached cheek. "Not that I'll weep very long for little Sal," he muttered half to himself. "D'you know that five million he offered me was *counterfeit*? I thought it had a funny smell. . . ."

"Who iced them . . . ?" Reeves's brow knit in perplexity. "Good lord," he blurted, "haven't you been reading the papers? It's *Batman*!"

The Joker straightened to his full height and lifted his right hand palm out. Strapped to his glove was a tiny joy buzzer. He pressed the central button with his middle finger and an angry buzz sounded in the office. *"Wrong!"* He wagged his forefinger at Reeves. "It most definitely *ain't* the Bat."

"But—" Reeves was astounded.

"Nope, nope, nope." The attenuated clown face shook rapidly from side to side. Then he thrust his head forward, tugging at the bottom of one black-rimmed eye to make it bulge from its socket. "I've *seen* the guy, Artie. He looks more like the ghost of Christmas future than our pointy-eared pal. Nowhere near as cute as Batboy."

Reeves stared at the Joker with an expression of incomprehension. He tilted his head to the side, his face skeptical. "Wait. You're saying it was someone else?"

The Joker matched the angle of Reeves's head with his own, bringing his grotesque face close to the other man's. "And they told me you were slow! Yeah, Artie, that's exactly what I'm sayin'. Someone who wouldn't mind seeing our dear old pals out of the way." The scarlet lower lip quivered in make-believe sorrow. "Maybe even—gulp, sob—me, too." He turned away from the councilman with a dramatic flourish and buried his face in his hands. "And that's when I thought about you, *cher* Arturo." He swiveled his head around, the false sorrow replaced by a look of guile. "An important, upstanding guy like you might find it a tad awkward if certain info came to light regarding his sordid past." He stalked back toward the desk.

"Hey, wait." Beaumont backed away as the clown marched toward him. "You're not saying that you think *I*—"

MASH OF THE PHANTASM

A loud buzz interrupted his protestations. The Joker looked down at his right palm in apparent befuddlement, then pointed his cane at the small speaker on Reeves's desk top. "Phone, little Artie." He used the tip of the cane to jab a button on the intercom.

Reeves swallowed nervously from the other side of the desk. "Y-yes?"

"Mr. Reeves?" said his secretary. "Miss Beaumont on the line."

"Thank you, Robert," Reeves started to say. "But—"

"Beaumont?" The Joker stared at the red light winking at the base of the small device. "Not the babe?" He flashed Reeves a sly look. "Oh, Art, you devil, you!" He lifted his cane again and hit the second button.

"Arthur?" Reeves lunged for the phone at the sound of Andrea's voice. The clown blocked him expertly and yanked him back from the desk, raising a long, white-gloved finger to his scarlet leer. "Shhh!" He giggled silently, a wayward child about to perpetrate a phone prank. His eyes were filled with cold menace.

Reeves swallowed. "Hello, Andrea." He struggled to keep the agitation from his voice. "We're still on for lunch, right?"

"I'm sorry, Arthur, I got hung up." Background noises revealed that Andrea was speaking from the phone in her convertible. "Let's make it dinner—say, eight o'clock? I'll explain everything tonight, okay?"

Reeves turned to look at the Joker. The clown bobbed his long face up and down.

BATMAN: THE ANIMATED MOVIE

"All right, Andrea. Fine. I'll see you then."

The connection went dead. The Joker lifted his arm and circled it wildly in the air before slamming his index finger down on the speaker button. He turned to Reeves, who was cringing away from the violent gestures. "Now ain't that just a co-inky-dink?" the clown drawled. He bolted suddenly forward and grabbed Reeves by the lapels. "Here we are gabbin' about the old man, and the veritable spawn of his loins just happens to call."

Lightning flashed in the storm outside, casting the Joker's arcane shadow over Reeves's face as the clown loomed above him, forcing him gradually to his knees. "Heh-heh, makes you want to laugh out loud—doesn't it, Artski?" The tall man hauled Reeves up from the carpet and swung him around, then shoved him down hard onto the desk top. He raised his long arm and struck the struggling councilman once, savagely, crazy laughter bubbling through his gritted teeth. Thunder mixed with the Joker's rising laughter as Reeves fell back motionless against the desk top. Soon there were other sounds.

THIRTY

For a while the laughter had competed with the modulated blare of the ambulance siren. Now it filled the hospital room, unchallenged.

Councilman Arthur Reeves, dressed in a pale green hospital gown, rolled back and forth on the bed, his body spasming uncontrollably with wave after wave of gasping laughter. Reeves's handsome face was twisted into a painful rictus. Veins bulged on his forehead and his hands twitched.

Doctor Morton Denquel stood by, an intern and a nurse at his back. The nurse held a tray with a syringe and a small bottle of clear fluid.

Denquel extended a dark hand behind him. The intern filled the syringe and passed it to him.

"Councilman, please!" The doctor hovered at the side of the thrashing man, waiting for an opportunity to administer the injection. "You've got to control yourself!"

Reeves's eyes bulged with pain and terror above the

huge grin. "I'm trying," he choked out between laughing gasps. "For god's sake, can't you see I'm trying!"

The nurse took a step closer to the bed. Just then Reeves's arms flailed wildly, knocking the tray from her hands. Gritting her teeth she leaned down onto the bed, helping the intern pin the councilman down while the doctor gave him the shot. Reeves's laughter began to subside almost at once. He sagged back onto the bed, his chest heaving weakly.

The nurse bent to retrieve the tray and bottle from beneath the bed.

"There." Doctor Denquel handed the syringe back to the intern. "That should relax you enough for the toxin to run its course. It's vital that you try to stay calm."

"Okay," Reeves gasped, his eyelids drooping. "Okay . . ."

The doctor and his entourage exited the room.

Reeves closed his eyes and gave in to the crushing fatigue. Two minutes later a small sound tugged at his attention. He rolled over to see a tall, dark figure slide into the room through the window. "Oh, n-no . . ." he said weakly. Then he giggled.

The dark shape loomed over the bed.

"Why did the Joker meet with you?" The voice was husky, a grim whisper.

"No . . ." Reeves shook his head from side to side, his mouth stretching out into a panicked grin as tears began to form at the corners of his eyes. Another giggle escaped his lips.

The threatening shape leaned closer. "It has to do

MASK OF THE PHANTASM

with the gangster murders, doesn't it? He thinks you're involved." The black mask dipped to within inches of Reeves's trembling face. *"Why?"*

Tears streamed from the councilman's eyes as he fought to keep himself from laughing. "I—I don't know."

The Dark Knight yanked Reeves up off the bed by the front of his gown. His eyes were narrow slits in the mask. "That's *not* the answer I want."

Terrified, Reeves began to babble, his words interspersed with high-pitched giggles. Sweat beaded on his brow. "B-Beaumont needed me to help him— *ha!*—and his k-kid get out of town. He—*ha!*—he kept in touch."

"When was the last time you spoke to him?"

"Years ago." Reeves drew in a gasping breath. "My first election campaign. I was running out of money and—*ha!*—I asked Beaumont for help." He swallowed hard. "He said no."

Batman scowled, an expression of deepening disgust on his face. "So you sold him to the mob," he said grimly.

"I was broke! *Ha-ha!* Desperate!" The uncontrollable giggles had started again. "Th-they said all they w-wanted was their money b-back! *Ha!*" The councilman clamped his jaw shut with an effort of will, then burst into gales of wild laughter.

The Dark Knight opened his hands, dropping the roaring, thrashing Reeves back onto the bed like a lion releasing a hyena. He exited through the window, his black cape swirling, seconds before the door flew open and the doctor and his assistants rushed back into the room.

THIRTY-ONE

The bat-winged shape dropped from the night sky onto the balcony outside Andrea Beaumont's suite. He stood for a moment regarding his reflection in the polished glass, then tried the French doors. They were unlocked. Batman stepped into the dark bedroom and moved cautiously about, a shadow among shadows. He checked the top of the dresser, peered into the closet, then approached the desk.

Andrea's gold locket was lying on the desk top, illuminated by a sliver of moonlight. Batman picked up the locket and thumbed the release catch. The two halves sprung apart, revealing a small photo of a younger Bruce and Andrea. They were smiling at each other, the ocean at their backs, their hair tousled by the wind. Batman stared down at the picture, his face expressionless. He snapped the locket shut and set it down, the slender gold chain running like water through his black gloves to pool on the desk top. He turned away and headed back toward the balcony.

The phone gave an initial jangle and started to ring. Batman stopped, his hands on the door handles, and looked back over his shoulder. He moved to the phone and lifted the receiver from its cradle, then brought it to his ear and listened.

"Hel-*loooooo*—anybody home?" The Joker punctuated his question with a burst of chilling laughter. The Dark Knight's grip tightened on the receiver.

"Listen, Boopsie," the clown drawled, "even though you never remember to call or write, I still got a soft spot for you. So I'm sending you a little gift—*air mail*!"

Batman became aware of a low droning sound coming from the partially open French doors. He wheeled around and stared out over the balcony. Something was approaching through the darkness, a gradually expanding dot before the moon.

"Oh, by the way," the Joker cackled, "I wouldn't recommend jumping out the window this time. Ta-ta, Toots!" Faint, crazy laughter leaked out into the room as Batman dropped the receiver. He darted to the window and peered out, his heart racing.

Some sort of miniature aircraft was heading straight for the balcony. It had an old-fashioned, oddly familiar look to it. Then the Dark Knight recognized it as one of the little autogyros he had seen years ago at the Gotham World's Fair. Attached to the underside of the plane was a bomb the size of a watermelon, with wide eyes and a big shark's grin painted across its snout. As

BATMAN: THE ANIMATED MOVIE

Batman moved to the side, he saw that KA-BOOM! had been lettered in purple on the bomb's side.

The autogyro was a few yards from the balcony. Batman extracted a star-shaped object from his belt and hurled it at the wide-eyed grin. The batstar struck the bomb squarely on its nose. There was a flash of blinding light followed by a huge noise. Batman covered his head with his cape as the concussion shattered the French doors, sending shrapnel from the bomb and shards of broken glass sleeting across the room.

Smoke wreathed the suite. Batman rose cautiously, blinking at the bright afterimages. He picked his way over the rubble and approached the balcony, a batarang in his hand. The night sky was empty. At his back, the phone receiver hung off the edge of the upended desk, still swinging back and forth at the end of its coiled cord. "Hello?" came a faint voice. "Hello? Operator! I believe my party's been disconnected—or is the proper word dismembered?" Peals of tinny laughter followed the Dark Knight as he aimed his grappling gun into the night sky and fired.

THIRTY-TWO

Andrea Beaumont wandered as if through a dream in the silvery light of a moonlit fantasy landscape. She was only dimly aware of her surroundings as she mounted a wide ramp and passed beneath the shadows of strange and towering structures. Her blue-green eyes were haunted and her thoughts were somewhere miles away and long ago. . . .

The villa had been beautiful, their nicest home yet, a comfortable dwelling of stucco walls with a roof of curving terra-cotta tiles and lush gardens. It was not far from the village, and a long arm of the sea stretched at its back, calm and bright and unbelievably blue.

It was Thursday and she had been at the marketplace most of the afternoon. The late sun cast long shadows ahead of her as she carried her groceries in their cloth sacks up the wide marble steps.

BATMAN: THE ANIMATED MOVIE

She stood at the front door and balanced the groceries awkwardly, reaching for the handle, which was dull bronze and shaped like a lion's head. Before she could touch it, the knob turned on its own and the door opened inward.

"Da—" The word died on her lips as the man stepped out into the sunlight. He was tall and gaunt, with hooded eyes and a jaw that jutted above his collar. Andrea stared at him in shock, a sensation like cold fire prickling in her stomach.

"You!" She stumbled back a step, dislodging a tomato and a long loaf of crusty bread from the sack in her right arm. "But he *paid* you—"

Her eyes widened at the implications of the tall man's presence inside the villa. She dropped the sacks on the doorstep and hurled herself past him.

The tall man grinned his wide grin. He plucked a handkerchief from his breast pocket and used it to wipe his prints from the doorknob, then stuffed the cloth back into his pocket and adjusted it carefully. He glanced down at the scattered groceries and stooped to pick an apple from the steps. He shined it on his lapel as he continued nonchalantly down the stairs. "Afternoon, Miss Beaumont," he said softly, waggling a thin eyebrow at the apple. "Hope you didn't bother to shop for two. . . ." His laughter climbed into the afternoon sunlight, almost—but not quite—drowning out the screams that came from inside the villa.

Andrea lifted her head in the moonlight. Her face was bleak as she looked around. She was sitting at the base of a huge circular object, a rusted sphere of painted metal. She wiped a single small tear from her cheek and got to her feet. Then she turned and moved toward the vast dome of the world of the future, the sorrow in her eyes replaced by a fierce resolve.

THIRTY-THREE

The sound of metal striking wood came as regularly as a metronome. The android stood straight-backed at the small countertop, its tireless arm rising and falling relentlessly above the scarred surface.

"Out, Rusty!" The man who reclined on the threadbare couch suddenly uncrossed his long legs, leaned over, and hurled what had once been a mechanical dog through the air. There was a crash of machinery as the remains of the small robot sailed into a concrete pylon and dropped to the floor. The Joker stretched to his feet, paused to scratch his sides with a hearty yawn, and hopped across the tracks that divided the living room from the kitchen in the House of the Future.

He sauntered over to stand close behind the android. "Well, Hazel." He rested his white-gloved hand on the pivoting shoulder. "I guess it's about time to call it a night." He was carrying a long salami tucked under his right arm. Placing it on the counter-

MASK OF THE PHANTASM

top, he pushed it slowly forward under the android's chopping knife until half a dozen slices had been cut. He popped one into his mouth and chewed thoughtfully. "Whaddya say, hon?" he said around the slice of meat. He put his hands on the android's shoulders, then reached down and snaked an arm about its waist. "Feelin' the ol' electricity tonight?" He chuckled. He reached lower and closed his fingertips in a playful pinch, then brought his hand up and stared blankly at the large piece of foam padding that had come loose in his fingers. He tucked it into his breast pocket like a handkerchief and arranged it carefully.

A slight breeze lifted the tails of his purple coat. The Joker ran his hand over his slicked-back emerald locks and turned to frown at an open glass door at the rear of the diorama. Silvery curtains swayed slightly in the breeze. A hint of dark mist was swirling on the floor just inside the doorway.

The clown clucked his tongue against his teeth. "Ain't that always the way?" he muttered with a light pat on the android's shoulder. "Y'get in the mood and company pops in."

The mist grew in volume and darkness, rising into the room to form a thick, roiling column. A dark figure appeared at the center of the column and stepped forward into the living room. It was clad in black, with a ragged cloak and a pale skull mask. The dark wraith glared at the startled clown like doom personified.

"Joker . . ." The eerie voice reverberated in the room. *"Your angel of death awaits. . . ."*

"Huh." The clown scratched idly at his chest, then wagged his index finger at the looming figure. "I'm impressed, lady," he said. "You're harder to kill than a cockroach on steroids."

The apparition stood motionless. Then its gloved left hand came up slowly, pulling off the ragged cape and the death's head mask in one motion.

"So you figured it out." Andrea Beaumont gave her head a shake, freeing her long hair to stir in the breeze. Without the filtering mechanism of the skull mask, her voice sounded brittle, tense.

"Hey—gotta hand it to ya. Nice scheme." The Joker looked her up and down, rubbing his long jaw appraisingly. "Costume's a bit theatrical, and it hides that killer bod—but, hey, who am I to talk?"

He struck a dramatic pose, relaxed for a second, and aimed a powerful roundhouse punch directly at Andrea's chin. She waited till the last possible instant to nimbly sidestep the blow, then raised her left arm as the clown stumbled past her. Black smoke seemed to ripple like a living thing from the fingertips of her glove, enveloping the Joker's head. He stumbled away, coughing and gagging.

The mist clung tenaciously to his head as he ran blindly forward, his arms flailing in a frantic attempt to clear it from his eyes. He collided heavily with the back wall of the kitchen and swayed there groggily. He bent over at the waist, coughing hoarsely for a few moments as the tenebrous mist began to dissipate. "Cute, very cute." He gave Andrea a poisonous look.

She raised the gleaming claw mounted on her right arm and moved in slowly.

"But I can blow smoke, too, Toots." The Joker straightened up against the wall with a grunt and

201

MASK OF THE PHANTASM

thrust out his chest. Greenish gas hissed outward from the fake carnation in his purple lapel.

At once, coils of black mist rose up to wreathe Andrea's body. The greenish vapor was absorbed harmlessly into the shadowy fog.

"Nice trick, sweetheart. You could teach ol' Batbrain a thing or two about becoming scarce." The Joker whipped his long head back and forth, searching in vain for his vanished antagonist.

Andrea appeared suddenly behind the Joker and sent him flying with a well-placed karate kick. The clown hit the floor hard and sprawled unmoving on the footworn linoleum. As Andrea bent cautiously above him, he flipped onto his back like a long-legged beetle. "I can see you prefer the stronger stuff," he snarled, hand twisting at his lapel. Acid spat out of the carnation in a poisonous-looking yellow stream.

Andrea threw up her arm to shield her face. The stream spurted against her gleaming gauntlet with a hissing sound. She blinked in surprise as the metal claw began to erode rapidly wherever the acid had splattered it. Horrified, she grabbed the tip of the weapon in her left hand and yanked it from her arm, flinging it to the floor as the deadly claw dissolved into a pool of molten slag.

The Joker had jumped to his feet. Taking advantage of the moment, he stepped in quickly and delivered a trio of vicious punches to Andrea's face, neck, and stomach. She fell backward with a cry of pain and slumped white-faced to the floor. The clown knelt over her, straddling her recumbent body as his hands sought her forearms, pinning them to the linoleum. He

BATMAN: THE ANIMATED MOVIE

lowered his grotesque face toward hers with a malicious chuckle.

Then Andrea's knee jabbed upward into his crotch. He shot back with a yelp of agony. Andrea kicked out, her boot catching him on the chin and sending him reeling back. He bumped up against the cylindrical counter where the android continued its interminable chopping and sagged to his knees.

"You're not smiling, Joker." Andrea hopped to her feet and stalked toward the moaning clown. "I thought you found death amusing."

"Me?" Breathing heavily, he leaned on the edge of the counter and pulled himself to his feet. He backed away, pushing pieces of futuristic furniture at her in his wake. "Oh, never." He slid past the streamlined refrigerator and encountered another countertop, groped behind his back, and seized a portable power mixing machine with wicked-looking blades. He pressed the On button. "You won't hear a giggle out of me!" he exclaimed, darting toward his adversary with the whirring mixer extended in front of him like a high-tech saber. Andrea blocked the thrust of the spinning blades and kicked out expertly, sending the clown lurching back across the room.

The Joker's shoulder bumped up against a smooth panel, and his white-gloved hand crawled down over a series of switches like a frantic spider. His finger stabbed at a round red button.

On the other side of the kitchen, Hazel the android paused for half a second at its labors, its eyes glowing bright red as a jury-rigged relay closed inside it and peals of laughter came from the wire grille that cov-

MASK OF THE PHANTASM

ered the lower half of its face. The tempo of its chopping increased.

Andrea whipped around in anticipation of an attack from behind.

"Ha!" The Joker stretched back his arm and hurled the power mixer at her. "Made ya look!" he yelled. Andrea started to turn back, but the heavy mixer struck her on the shoulder, dropping her to her knees with a stunned groan. The Joker pressed a second button and Hazel rotated away from the chopping table, the long cleaver slashing empty air as glowing eyes focused on the fallen Andrea.

Gliding on a trio of tiny wheels, the deadly automaton advanced on Andrea. The young woman pushed raggedly to her feet. Stepping quickly backward, she ducked as the android's knife swept the air above her head, then darted in to kick Hazel off its wheels.

Squeeeee! As the robot collapsed in a clatter of old equipment, Andrea gave its chassis another kick, sending the defunct machine sliding across the room to where its master watched.

A piece of the disintegrating junk caught the clown's ankle as he stepped to one side. He teetered back against the chopping table. Andrea was on him in a second, her arms raised. She struck him repeatedly, landing a series of solid blows to his face and body. The Joker groped behind him on the table. His fingers brushed against the edge of a sharp cleaver— then closed around a much more substantial weapon.

"Ha! *En garde*!" Andrea reeled back as the Joker hit her on the side of the head with what was left of his dinner, the salami coming down hard on her cheek and temple. He struck her again, then dropped the sausage and vaulted across the tracks to the futuristic living room. As Andrea staggered dazedly after him, the clown ran straight for the huge picture window. He crashed through the glass in a shower of sharp fragments, stepped to the edge of the curving balcony and leaped off, his manic laughter fading into the darkness.

Andrea stepped through the broken glass and leaned out over the balcony. She tried to slow her breathing, conscious of the pounding of her pulse in her ears. The deserted fairgrounds spread out before her, nothing moving that she could see but a semicircle of silvery flags flapping raggedly in the breeze.

Directly in front of her stood the remains of the gigantic transportation exhibit: the atrophied skeleton of the partially disassembled monorail track, a colossal Ferris wheel in the shape of an automobile tire, a car battery the size of a small house, and a giant turbine propeller.

She leaned back from the railing with a look of grim determination. Clouds of dark smoke began to billow up around her black-clad form. When the mist cleared she was gone.

THIRTY-FOUR

A great puff of dark vapor appeared from nowhere on the ground near the base of the gigantic turbine. Andrea stepped forward as the smoke thinned. She scanned the nearby exhibits and began to walk slowly in the direction of the huge tire, the mist clinging to her costume like a protective shield as she moved.

"Well, well," came a familiar voice from the shadows. "If it ain't Smokey the babe—all misty-eyed and just in time to meet her biggest fan!"

Andrea looked off into the darkness, then turned and stared as the giant propeller came to life in front of her. It turned slowly at first, with a tired, creaking noise—then it gave voice to a deep-throated thrum as it rapidly picked up speed.

Small bits of debris began to roll and slide toward the huge fan. Andrea stumbled forward a few steps. The prop turned faster and faster, howling as it produced an intake suction of hurricane proportions. Her concealing fog was stripped away, and she dug in her heels and braced herself against the rising gale.

"*Tch.* She still seems a little down." The Joker crouched in the shadows of a ramshackle concession stand off to the right, a portable control mechanism in his white-gloved hands. He gave a sharp twist to one of the dials. "So how 'bout a little pick-me-up?"

The suction increased dramatically. Andrea was pulled forward in a succession of small hopping steps, as she fought the wind currents and tried to keep her footing. At last she grabbed one of the guy wires trailing from the giant car battery display, as she lost the battle and felt herself being lifted bodily into the air. Debris pummeled her. The wire held for half a minute before ripping free of its mooring. Andrea shot through the air, slamming into one of the metal struts of a smaller ride made up of six cars circling a twenty-foot spark plug topped with an array of tin lightning bolts. She searched vainly for handholds on the slippery metal, then the wind tugged her loose and she was airborne again. She forced herself to concentrate, twisting in midair and flinging out her arms as she flew toward a slender flagpole standing a scant several yards in front of the giant turbine. Her hands closed on its cold surface and she held on for dear life, her long hair streaming out along her back toward the spinning blades.

The Joker shook his head with a chuckle. "And people say the World's Fair isn't entertaining enough for the modern audience!" He edged the control dial up another notch. The thrumming of the turbine increased to a deafening roar. Andrea clung desperately to the flagpole, which was beginning to nod slowly in the direction of the giant fan.

Then a sleek black motorcycle zoomed into view. Batman streaked past the World of the Future and skidded to a halt at the edge of the windstream. He planted his boots on the pavement and scanned the immediate area. He stiffened when he caught sight of Andrea, her hands clutched around the flagpole as the tall shaft bent inexorably toward the deadly turbine.

The Dark Knight gunned the motor and shot forward toward the base of the flagpole. As he entered the heart of the windstream, the Batcycle began to drift sideways. He slewed the cycle around, heading directly into the stream as he revved the motor and raced forward. In a few seconds he had begun to outrace the pull of the windstream.

"What? The nerve of some buttinskis!" The Joker grimaced in fury, sticking his head around the corner of his hiding place behind the ruined concession stand. He lifted the remote control again and yanked the dial completely to the right. The song of the turbine climbed to a higher pitch.

Out on the pavement, the Batcycle began to wobble. Inside his hiding place, the clown grinned maliciously. Maybe he could kill two flying rodents with one stone!

Andrea's hands were numb. She could feel her grip weakening. As the Batcycle shot beneath her, her hands were ripped free of the flagpole and she was swept through the air toward the turbine. Batman looked up. As he continued his race toward the giant fan, the suction became powerful enough to lift the

Batcycle from the pavement. The Dark Knight clenched his jaw and headed the cycle up the wide steps that led to the turbine. At that moment the cycle and its rider became airborne. Batman rose high in the seat and kicked off from the pedals, sending the motorcycle careening ahead of him.

The Batcycle smashed directly into the fan. The metal framework at the front of the turbine buckled inward, and fragments of twisted machinery sprayed outward as the great mechanism collapsed in upon itself. Andrea and Batman both plunged to the ground as the windstream dwindled and died. Smoking debris rained down after them.

"You're *kidding*!" The Joker leapt to his feet behind the shell of the concession stand. "I've got half a mind to demand a refund on admission." He stood with hands on hips, surveying the destruction with outrage. Then he clucked his tongue and ducked back into the shadows.

Andrea got shakily to her feet. Her face was smeared with soot and covered with deep scratches. Her black costume was ripped in several places. She turned as a shadow fell on her.

Batman's face was grim beneath the black mask.

"Your father's dead, isn't he, Andrea?" His voice had a steely undertone that belied its calm. "You snuck into town to get Chuckie Sol, took off, and made your official arrival a few days later. That way you could shift the blame onto your father if you had to."

She looked up at him silently for a moment, her marvelous eyes unreadable.

"They took everything, Bruce. My dad. My life."
She paused. "You."

She looked away, faltering under his gaze. "I'm not
saying it's right," she continued through clenched
teeth. "I'm not even saying it's sane. But it's all I've
got left." She turned back, her eyes pleading for un-
derstanding. "So either help me or get out of my
way."

"You know I can't do that." He moved closer, his
hands moving restlessly at his sides.

"You can't do that?" Andrea gave a cry of pure
anguish. "Look what they *did* to us, Bruce! What we
could have had!" He recoiled slightly as she leaned
toward him, her fists clenching. "Oh, Bruce—they
had to *pay*!"

He felt something tearing inside. He lifted his hands
and placed them tenderly on her shoulders. "But,
Andi," he asked her softly, "what will vengeance
solve?"

She looked up at him, her eyes dry and empty. "If
anyone knows the answer to that, Bruce—it's you."

Stung, he released her. A deep sadness was welling
up inside him. He controlled it with an effort, his face
hardening with resolve.

"Leave, Andi," he said. "Now. Please."

She stared at him impassively for the space of a few
heartbeats. Dark, billowing mist appeared behind her,
enveloping her completely as she stepped back into its
heart.

His shoulders slumping forward, the Dark Knight
stood staring into the mist until it began to clear. He

was alone. A cold, hard look came into his eye. He turned toward the concession stand and headed off.

He hadn't been walking for very long when he heard a shrill whistle. He looked up. A figure in a purple coat stepped out from behind a pillar about a hundred yards in front of him. It waved foppishly.

"Over heeeeere!" The Joker ducked back behind the pillar.

Batman raced forward. Up ahead, the clown checked back over his purple shoulder to make sure he was being followed, then disappeared into the entrance to the World of the Future exhibit.

Batman walked slowly into the dark building. He found himself facing the huge, silent model of the City of the Future. There was a scraping noise, which seemed to come from in front of him. He paused at the edge of the city, then stepped cautiously over the low barrier and walked out into the lifeless metropolis.

He surveyed the model. The tallest skyscrapers stood a good six feet above his head. He prowled through empty streets and stepped over parks and ponds. He crossed an arching bridge, his senses alert. As he turned his eyes toward the mock-Gotham's lower east side a strange thing happened. Behind his back, the top of a streamlined-looking building shuddered slightly and then moved a few inches to the left. The migrating edifice stopped when Batman glanced its way, slid sideways again when he turned his head, and then froze into immobility as his eyes wandered west.

The Joker had removed the top four stories of one of the model buildings and fitted it over his head. Underneath the bizarre facade, he grinned as the Dark Knight searched the dead city. He held another small remote in his hand.

When he pressed a button, the entire city came to life around them, lights spreading outward from the center and miniature vehicles beginning to move in preprogrammed traffic patterns. Startled, Batman looked up as buildings lit up to his left and right, then he grimaced as a tractor trailer crashed into his heel. A diminutive schoolbus rammed into the back of the trailer, followed by a garbage truck and a three-inch limousine. Traffic was piling up around his feet. He was beginning to understand how Gulliver must have felt in Lilliput. Then a building moved behind him.

The Joker reared up suddenly, yanked the model building from his head and bashed it down hard on Batman's skull.

The Dark Knight fell forward, striking a model train depot. The clown laughed above him, raising the chunk of building back over his head and pointing it spire first at his fallen foe. Batman raised his eyes just in time to see the foot-long spike plunging down toward him. He rolled to one side. The Joker chortled gleefully.

"Clash of the titans, eh, Batman?" the clown sneered. "Or, in your case, the cretin!"

Batman fired a swift kick at the jutting white jaw. The Joker slammed back into a multistory office building, staggering to the side as the model crumbled under his weight. The Dark Knight loomed ominously in front of him.

"Joker." The word sounded like a curse.

BATMAN: THE ANIMATED MOVIE

"Guilty." The Joker chuckled. There was a tooth missing on the left side of his contorted smile. His long nose had begun to bleed. He wiped it casually on his purple sleeve. Then he whipped out the small control box and pointed it at his foe. There was the click of a tiny switch.

Nothing happened. Batman backed away, looking warily to left and right. He turned at a familiar droning sound growing behind him.

He saw the first autogyro as it soared into view around a skyscraper at the other end of the city. Then a second appeared behind it, and a third. He counted four in all: a miniature invasion fleet droning toward him above the model city.

The Joker gave a high-pitched laugh and scurried off on hands and knees. Batman was turning to follow him when pain slashed suddenly through his left shoulder. The lead plane had darted forward, slicing his upper arm with its razor-sharp rotor. The Dark Knight spun around to face his attackers as two more dived at him. He ducked and dodged as they buzzed around him like a swarm of gigantic bees.

Several streets away, the Joker popped back into view. His head and shoulders moved rapidly along the skyline, as if he were on roller skates. When he suddenly emerged from behind the concealment of the buildings, he was standing on the back of a small commuter train. The clown leaped from the string of cars as they mounted a bridge that curved around the make-believe waterfront. He landed on a tiny wharf and picked his way among the smaller buildings to the side of a domed stadium. Lifting the dome with a grunt of effort, he reached down with his long arm until his hand encountered the power switch he had hidden there months before.

What remained of Hazel the android lay on its back, eyes flashing redly, on the linoleum kitchen floor of the House of the Future. The mechanical housewife was still slashing fitfully with its one good arm at the empty air next to the large chrome-and-enamel oven recessed into one of the counters. Inside the oven, a white kitchen timer sat atop a stout pyramid constructed of sticks of dynamite. The moment after the Joker threw his hidden switch inside the dome of the model stadium, the timer began to count slowly backwards.

THIRTY-FIVE

Batman ducked and swerved, as the fleet of autogyros attacked in what he was coming to realize was a carefully choreographed battle maneuver. Frustrated, he swatted at one of the little planes. Breath hissed in through his teeth as another swooped low across his back, slashing down through his cape and uniform. He whirled around angrily, blood starting to drip from a wound just below his right cheekbone. One of the small planes chose that moment to dive kamikaze-style straight for his face. The Dark Knight waited till the last instant, then knotted his fist and scored a direct hit on the autogyro's nose. Pain throbbed through his hand as the plane was knocked off course, wobbled its wings, and smashed into the ground. He looked up and prepared to repeat the maneuver as a second plane began its dive.

The last two seemed to have learned from their comrades' mistakes. They took turns circling warily just outside the reach of his fist. Finally, he unfastened his tattered cape from his shoulders and flung it out like a matador. The little planes were caught in the dark folds. Batman swung the cape heavily against the side of a nearby art museum, demolishing both the building and the autogyros. He stood for a moment, breathing deeply and holding his slashed shoulder. Then he swung the cape up from the base of the museum, scattering broken autogyro parts as he settled it back across his shoulders. He grimaced as a falling fuselage brushed his wounded arm. Then he turned, his fists clenching again as the sound of raucous laughter echoed down over the city.

"You're too late, Barfman." The clown stood on a viewing causeway high above the miniature city. "There are twenty miles of tunnels under these fair fairgrounds—and they're all chockful of high explosives! In five petite minutes, everything goes up in the biggest blast since last year's Arkham Asylum Christmas party!" He turned with a bow and sprinted back along the causeway toward the building's exit.

Batman took off in hot pursuit, leaping over municipal buildings and scaling skyscrapers until he was able to swing up onto the causeway and race after the fleeing figure. The causeway ended at a large door that opened onto a dark tunnel. Batman ran through the twisting corridor, led only by the eerie sound of the Joker's laughter, which floated back continually from somewhere up ahead. At length the corridor terminated in a half-open door. Batman grabbed the handle and flung the door wide.

He was suddenly outside. He looked about suspiciously in the moonlight. Blood was dripping from his injured shoulder and the pain was growing more intense. Then he heard a sound like a great engine warming up. It was coming from the other side of the building. He made his way slowly to the edge of the structure and stepped around the corner.

In front of him was a statue of a spaceman. A large spaceman. It soared well over a hundred feet from the thick boots to the hand upraised in stylized greeting. The faceless figure had a bubble helmet on its head, and a cumbersome rocket pack was strapped to its monumental back. Batman's eyes flicked downwards. Something had moved near one of the spaceman's feet. He squinted in the moonlight and made out the figure of the Joker. The clown was in the act of fastening the strap on his own helmet.

On his back, the Joker was wearing a scaled-down version of the spaceman's giant rocket pack. The roaring noise was the sound of the pack's engines being revved. The clown shot Batman an evil grin and grabbed the throttle of the flying device. He took a few steps away from the statue's foot, the whine of the engine growing louder. He gave Batman a jaunty wave.

Flames gushed from the rocket nozzles. Dust from the pavement boiled up in the wake of his exhaust as the rocket pack lifted him trembling into the air. The Dark Knight scowled and sprinted toward the statue.

The Joker laughed gleefully as he rose in wavering flight past the colossal spaceman's knee, then his belt, and then his blank helmet. Batman raced across the pavement far below him, craning his neck to keep his

MASK OF THE PHANTASM

adversary in sight. The clown leveled off at the height of the spaceman's shoulder. He circled the giant figure a few times to get the feel of the controls, then angled his flight toward the huge rusted globe and rocketship that had once formed the fair's centerpiece. Batman followed below, his breathing labored and his eyes narrowed in pain. The Joker hovered near the great sphere as if conducting a casual inspection. Below, the Dark Knight leaped onto the tail of the canted rocket and half ran, half climbed skyward.

The clown dawdled by the rocket's nose, still cackling loudly to himself. Batman looked up, calculated swiftly, and jumped up onto the slippery metal cone. He paused momentarily to steady himself, then contracted his legs and shot upward again just as the rusted nose collapsed with a shriek of metal under his weight.

"Hey!" cried the clown, genuinely surprised as the Dark Knight landed high on his back. They struggled, the rocket pack veering out of control. The hem of Batman's cape caught fire briefly, then was snuffed out by the rushing wind, as they wheeled and dived through the dark sky. The Joker twisted left and right in an attempt first to dislodge his unwanted passenger, and then to fry him in the exhaust from the rockets.

They shot out over the fairgrounds. A bridge was approaching rapidly and the Joker descended toward it. Midway under the shallow arch, the clown wrenched up on the controls, smashing the Dark Knight into the concrete. Stunned, Batman felt his grip loosening. The Joker reached back and grabbed him, his long fingers digging deep into his enemy's

BATMAN: THE ANIMATED MOVIE

wounded shoulder. Batman grimaced in pain and swung around to the front of the Joker's body, clinging face to face to the clown's shoulders.

"You just don't know when to quit, do you?" the Joker grated through his tight smile. He clawed at the masked man's face, trying to gouge his eyes. Batman hooked his left arm around the Joker's neck and held on tight. He raised his right fist and delivered a series of short jabs to the side of the other man's face. The rocketmen careened out of control, passing perilously close to the towering exhibits.

"You're crazy!" the clown screamed. "I'm your only chance to get out of here alive!" He rammed the flat of his gloved hand against the Dark Knight's face and pushed with all his strength.

Batman's black glove closed around the Joker's white one. He contracted his fingers with crushing force around the other hand. "That's the *idea*!" Batman snarled into the clown's panicked face. He released his hold for an instant, then yanked viciously on the harness of the rocket pack. They spiraled downward toward the pavement with Batman in control.

The Joker shrieked in terror as they swooped down, changed direction abruptly, and arced upward through a steel archway with inches to spare. They were heading straight toward the central sphere. The Joker's scream grew louder.

The two men struck the Omniglobe at an angle, punching through the corroded metal. They punched a second hole and shot out again near the base of the sphere, striking hard against the pavement beneath it. The two bodies flew apart.

MASH OF THE PHANTASM

The jets sputtered and died. For a few heartbeats everything was silent.

Batman moved first. He pushed up on his elbows, trying to catch his breath. His chest heaved in great gasps.

Then the Joker stirred. Moaning, he struggled to a sitting position and clawed weakly at the rocket pack still fastened to his back. The buckles parted and the pack fell away. The battered clown glanced over at Batman, summoning a woozy smile. "Well," he mumbled. "How about that? For once, I'm stuck without a punch line. . . ."

A shadow fell across the pavement beyond his feet. He looked up, his face filling with comic dread.

Andrea Beaumont stepped into the moonlight and grabbed the Joker by his purple collar. She dragged him to his feet with a grunt.

"Okay, okay!" The exhausted criminal raised his hands in a limp parody of surrender. He managed a hoarse chuckle. "I give up already. . . ."

Several yards away, the Dark Knight staggered to his feet.

"Oh, *Bat*man!" The Joker's voice held a hint of panic. He looked back over his shoulder at the other man. "I surrendered—*you* heard me. Tell her, Batman!"

"Andrea!" Batman called. "You've got to get out of here! He's put dynamite under the fairgrounds—the whole place is wired to explode!"

"No." Andrea looked from the Dark Knight's bruised and bleeding face to the cringing clown she held in front of her. "One way or another, it ends tonight." Her expression softened as she raised her eyes to Batman once more. "Good-bye, my love."

He stood facing them, despair in his eyes. "Andrea . . ."

All was calm and orderly in the kitchen of the House of the Future. A steady, muffled ticking came from inside the recessed oven. A large chunk of the robot dog lay on its side at the base of a pylon, yapping softly from time to time as distant noises activated its program. Its android mistress was chopping the air less swiftly now than in minutes past, the swings of the corroded arm growing more and more erratic as tiny gears and sprockets popped from its elbow joints and rolled across the linoleum.

Then the steady ticking stopped. A shrill ringing sound came from inside the oven.

A half-second later, the house exploded in a great flash of orange light. Five seconds after that, another, larger explosion took place several meters directly beneath the first one, triggering a series of underground detonations that radiated outward from the World of the Future like ripples on a lake. The earth buckled.

Cars shaped like stylized bolts of lightning flew from their cables as the ground erupted beneath the spark plug ride. The Ferris wheel that had been fashioned in the shape of an enormous tire was nudged from its base. With a terrible creaking sound, it began to roll toward the monorail track. The track crumpled like a foil ribbon when the tire struck it. The runaway Ferris wheel plowed on into the side of the Forward to the Future building. The vast dome shuddered under the impact and collapsed inward like an imploding egg.

Explosions were occurring everywhere. The faceless spaceman, his arm still raised in optimistic salute, toppled forward and disappeared in a fountain of dust and fire. The Omniglobe and the Astroplane were also in flames, paint peeling and plastic cracking as black smoke roiled upwards.

Still clutching the Joker, Andrea turned with a look of childlike wonder to stare up at the magnificent blaze.

A tiny chuckle escaped the clown's contorted mouth, and then another. The scarlet lips parted and peals of insane laughter spilled forth as Andrea turned back to him. Flaming debris was beginning to rain down all around them. The Joker's hysterical laughter grew even wilder as she raised her black-gloved hand.

Batman staggered toward Andrea, forcing his exhausted legs to work by pure willpower. He cried out as clouds of dark mist began to billow up around her and the howling villain. The laughter built to a crescendo as the mist enfolded them, then stopped abruptly.

"Andrea!" He threw himself forward into the mist and found nothing but shadows. He gave a choking cough as smoke from the blazing exhibits swirled down to mix with the dissipating mist. He stumbled back through the charred debris. Then the burning centerpiece exploded with a roar, sending out a wall of intense heat to break over him like a wave. He flung his arms up to protect his face and took a blind step backward. The ground opened up beneath him.

BATMAN: THE ANIMATED MOVIE

He fell into a frigid chaos. There was darkness and movement and the sound of rushing water. He had the sense of being drawn along a massive tunnel whose walls were collapsing behind him. He searched for the surface as he felt his consciousness slipping away, finally bursting out into the air just in time to be plunged down and over a great height. The water whirled all around him, cold, numbing. It took a mighty effort for him to relax, no longer fighting the current, but letting it take him where it would.

It took him to a shallow estuary. He floated for a while under the moonlight, glad to be breathing. Finally he found something solid beneath his boots and crawled to his feet. There was a great orange glow in the sky to his right. He stood and watched the final moments of the cataclysm.

              The cavern was silent, the majority of its inhabitants having departed some time ago to hunt the black skies until dawn.

The two men faced each other in the dimness, neither looking in the other's eyes. The gray costume was ripped in a score of places, burned in others. The black cowl lay on a nearby rock shelf, on top of what was left of the black cape. The body had suffered as badly as the costume. Scratches and bruises competed for space on his smoke-darkened skin. One leg was splinted, one eye swollen shut.

"I couldn't save her, Alfred." Bruce lifted his fist, clenched it, then let it fall limply to his side. He raised his eyes to the older man.

"I don't think she wanted to be saved, sir," the butler told him in a gentle voice. He set down the silver tray that held bottles and bandages and rested his hand lightly on his friend's shoulder. "Vengeance blackens the soul, Bruce. It was always my secret fear that you might become that which you fought against. You walk on the edge of that abyss every night that you emerge from this cave, I think—but you've never fallen in. And I thank heaven for that.'' He shook his gray head at the anguish in the other man's face. ''Andrea fell into that pit years ago. And no one—not even you—could have pulled her out.''

Bruce looked away. The words had the ring of truth, but the truth was small comfort at this hour. From the corner of his eye, he caught the dance of a tiny sparkle of light.

Frowning, he stood and limped into the shadows. Alfred was watching him with a puzzled look. ''What is it, Master Bruce?''

A fang of limestone descended some thirty feet from the unseen ceiling, narrowing to a nubbled point a few feet above a horizontal slab of rock. Something small and bright and golden hung from its tip.

Bruce reached out and lifted the locket into his trembling hand. He turned back to Alfred and held it up to catch the light, his face filled with wonder.

THIRTY-SEVEN

It was taking Burt a bit longer than he had expected to get his sea legs. He stood in a corner of the big ballroom and sipped cautiously at his champagne as he watched the revelers. A golden paper crown was perched lopsidedly on his head, given to him by the same pair of giggling young women who had told him that champagne was good for seasickness. His stomach gave a warning lurch as the ship moved on the swell of a slow wave.

Burt set down his drink and walked unsteadily across the ballroom. Maybe the salt air would help settle his stomach. He slipped out into the darkness and made his way across the deck to the railing.

It was hard for him to believe how much his life had changed in such a short time. It had started when he stopped in at the Kwik-shot to pick up his pictures after his second day of work in Crime Alley. Maggie had advanced him his first week's salary from the

BATMAN: THE ANIMATED MOVIE

Community Center to pay for them, and it had taken almost all of the check.

The photographs had come out beautifully clear and sharp with the tiny date-and-time stamp from his camera visible in the lower right hand corner of each picture. They had packed them in the envelope in reverse order, and Burt had stood on the pavement outside the store and thumbed through them slowly, lingering over the shots of his new friends and co-workers. Then he had reached the pictures from the hotel. He pursed his lips. The shots of the car had turned out very professional looking—though looking at them as he stood on the sidewalk outside the Kwik-shot made Burt feel kind of sad. It didn't seem fair to be driving your sports car out of a parking garage one moment, and then finding yourself dead and sticking out of the side of a hotel the next. Not even if you were a gangster. He slid the final photograph from the bottom of the pile and stared at it in consternation.

It took him five seconds to recognize the concrete wall of the garage, another ten to recall the startled instant when he had heard the car smash through the retaining wall and lowered the camera from his eyes, his finger squeezing tight on the button out of pure reflex. The camera had been aimed up toward the top of the garage when the shutter had clicked. He looked closely at the picture, his pulse racing.

The camera had caught the tilted edge of the parking garage wall, with the jagged gap where the silver sports car had sailed out into the air appearing perfectly centered in the photo. But it had caught something else, too.

MASK OF THE PHANTASM

Standing in the gap of the wall was a figure dressed all in black, with a long ragged cloak that flowed out behind it in the wind. Tongues of dark mist swirled around the figure—but the long, gleaming claw that stretched at the end of its right arm was clearly visible, as was the bone-colored death's head mask.

"It wasn't him," Burt muttered, looking up from the photo. "It *wasn't* Batman!" An elderly man passing by gave him a sidelong glance and quickened his pace.

He had hurried back to Park Row.

It was Dr. Thompkins who had convinced him to go to the newspaper himself, instead of just sending the photograph in anonymously. And it was Dr. T. who had given him a big hug of gratitude when he walked back into the center that night and presented her with the check the newspaper had given him. It had turned out that the newspaper was running a contest for photographers, and that Burt's picture had been declared the winner as soon as he turned it in. It was an awful lot of money, more than Burt had ever seen before and, as he had explained to Dr. T. and Maggie, there was nothing he could think of to do with it that could possibly bring him as much pleasure as giving it all to the center.

He had told them about his meeting with the chief editor of the *Gotham Times,* and about his other meeting with the police commissioner, a beaming, gray-haired man who had seemed very happy to meet him indeed. Other members of the center had come in while he was talking, and they had all gathered around him, listening to his story, sharing his delight.

BATMAN: THE ANIMATED MOVIE

The next morning, he had gone to the little news-stand outside his rented room feeling almost fearful. What if it had been a dream—or worse, a joke? Suppose they had decided not to run the picture, after all?

But there it was, front and center, under a big black double headline that read:

MYSTERY VILLAIN SNAPPED AT SCENE; AMATEUR SHUTTERBUG CLEARS BATMAN

Amateur shutterbug, Burt had thought, turning the words happily over in his mind. He had skimmed through the story, noting that the mystery villain, who had apparently left the city after the huge explosion at the fairgrounds, had been dubbed "the Phantasm" by one of the newspaper reporters. He flipped excitedly through the paper, discovering they had used another one of his photos where the story continued on page 2. A credit ran in tiny print up the side of each picture: PHOTOGRAPH BY B. EARNY.

Make that B. Earny, Amateur Shutterbug, he thought proudly.

Burt had purchased three copies of the *Times:* one to send to his parents, one to keep in his room, and one to have framed—because they had asked him— for his friends down at the center.

When he had showed up that morning they were waiting for him, all gathered together in the big room. After they had ooohed and ahhhed for a while about the newspaper, Dr. T. had presented him with the ticket they had gotten for him with some of the money.

MASK OF THE PHANTASM

Six days in the Caribbean, all expenses paid.

Burt had cried a little then, and tried to give it back, but none of them would hear of it. Maggie had told him his job would be waiting for him when he got back, and Dr. T. had promised that she wouldn't touch her file cabinet until he'd finished setting up his new system. Tansy had given him a hand-drawn picture of herself as Batwoman, and Miss Rosey had offered him detailed advice on where to find the best bargains in the Caribbean, which she seemed to think was somewhere off the coast of France. They had all come down to the dock that morning to see him off.

Burt leaned against the railing and stared out over the dark waters. His stomach had begun to calm down. His jaw was aching a little, and he realized with a start that it was probably sore from all the smiling he'd been doing lately. Some people on the ship had learned about his picture that evening, and everyone had wanted to congratulate him. Soon he had wanted nothing more than to be alone for the rest of the night. He tried another smile on, in spite of himself, and left it there. Some things were worth a little discomfort.

The moon slipped out from behind some high clouds, and he became aware of the woman standing silently by the railing about twenty feet down the deck. Her skirt and jacket were black, which was why he hadn't noticed her when he first came out.

Burt watched her for a few moments, beginning to rethink his decision to spend the rest of the evening by himself. She looked very alone standing there in front of the wide ocean, and it wouldn't hurt him to talk to one more person. He fumbled the paper crown

BATMAN: THE ANIMATED MOVIE

from his head and folded it into his back pocket. Then he smoothed back his hair and straightened his tie. He was wearing the one he had gotten himself for his last birthday, and he thought the Three Stooges looked very jolly with the moonlight hitting their wise, comical faces.

It was still a bit difficult to walk, thanks to the sea and the champagne, but he managed to make his way to a place not far from the woman without looking too tipsy. Suddenly shy, he turned and stared out over the ocean for almost a full minute before clearing his throat.

"It's quite a sight," Burt said finally, glancing at her profile. She was very beautiful, he realized. He looked at the play of moonlight on her cheekbones and wished that he could take her picture.

"Yes," the woman replied after a moment, giving him the barest nod. "Quite a sight." Her voice was soft, almost a whisper.

Burt waited another thirty seconds, not sure of the etiquette involved when meeting someone at sea. Then he moved a couple of steps closer and stuck out his hand. "Burton Earny," he said.

The woman made no response, staring out at the slow rise and fall of the waves as if she hadn't heard him. After a few seconds he allowed his hand to fall back to his side, feeling a little foolish. He was just trying to be friendly, after all. Then he looked more closely at her black garments, and at the expression of faraway sadness in her eyes. They were fascinating eyes, the kind of clear blue-green he had seen in the ocean this afternoon.

MASH OF THE PHANTASM

"I'm sorry," he said. "Have you . . . lost someone?"

At first he thought she was going to ignore him again. Her voice seemed to come from a very great distance when she answered him.

"Yes," she told him, "I have."

THIRTY-EIGHT

Night had returned to Gotham City. A bank of high clouds hid the stars, their bottom edges touched with the last pale gold of the hidden sun. A strong wind had come up from the west, fanning his long black cloak out behind him like a wing yearning for flight. He stood on the edge of a concrete precipice and looked down at the teeming city, a blur of shadows and colored lights.

A streak of yellow light lanced across the sky behind him. He lifted his head. A bright oval shuddered on the belly of the clouds, at its heart the image of a black bat suspended in mid-flight. He gazed at the wavering signal, black-gloved hands moving restlessly at his sides.

Then he unhooked the small gun from his belt and fired it into the darkness. The hook found purchase behind the pointed ear of a stone monster as a long slender cable trailed behind it. He grasped the line and swung out over the city, into the night.

ABOUT THE AUTHOR

GEARY GRAVEL is the author of *Shadows of the Past* and *Dual to the Death*, two novelizations based on BATMAN: THE ANIMATED SERIES. He has also written several science fiction books in two series, *The Autumnworld Mosaic* and *The Fading Worlds*.

Currently, Gravel devotes all of his time to writing, sleeping, and watching BATMAN: THE ANIMATED SERIES on television. His friends think he needs to get out more.

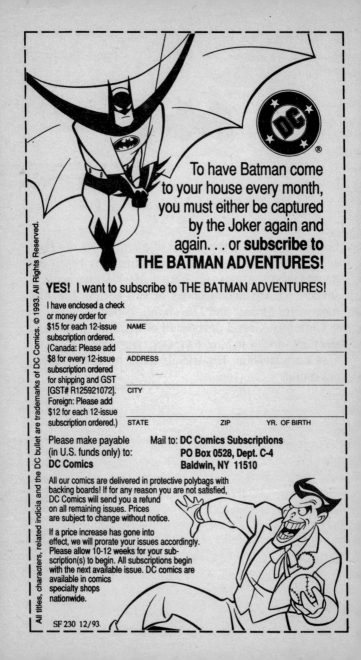